# AESTRANGEL

## THE

# RISEN

THE AESTRANGEL TRINITY

# AESTRANGEL

## THE RISEN

### Maria DeVivo

4 Horsemen
Publications, Inc.

4 Horsemen Publications, Inc.
1497 Main St. Suite 169
Dunedin, FL 34698
4horsemenpublications.com
info@4horsemenpublications.com

Cover by Niki Tantillo
Typesetting by Autumn Skye
Edited by Laura Mita



*Library of Congress Control Number: 2024933937*

*Paperback ISBN-13: 979-8-8232-0467-5*
*Hardcover ISBN-13: 979-8-8232-0468-2*
*Audiobook ISBN-13: 979-8-8232-0469-9*
*Ebook ISBN-13: 979-8-8232-0470-5*

# DEDICATION

For Joe - I would burn everything
to the ground for us if I had to.

For Jason - Your support and encouragement
mean the world to me. Family is not only blood.
You have always been and always will be my brother.

For Morgan - It's all for you and
will always be for you.

# TABLE OF CONTENTS

# PROLOGUE

For humankind, there had always been a balance. Evil lurked in every corner of their lives, but just waiting around the bend was salvation. Deception, heartache, loss, tragedy, and disease all peppered with success, friendship, fortune, and love... these were all mainstays of the human condition. But what was not understood was the need for balance in the universe. True balance. A balance that separated the pure and loving from the truly evil and demonic, not just the karmic under-linings of good vs. bad. Destructive forces threatened to overtake, and sweeping serenity would save the day. Humans were lulled by this thought. Comforted by the notion that no matter what happened in their lives, a new day would dawn.

This was the false sense of security all humans enjoyed...

...until Aestrangel showed them what true balance was almost halfway through the 21st century.

For the Lord had grown tired, and the Lord had grown weary, and the Lord had hated the subtle machinations of the good vs. the bad. Because at the end of the day, the tables always toppled over to his side.

But after the Evening Star rose up, there was pure darkness. A shadow of despair and hatred fell over the hearts of men and made the souls of women turn to stone. For two thousand years, Aestrangel inflicted upon the people a terror unprecedented in the history of mankind, for it is said that she could devour a person's spirit by just speaking their name.

She is the Dark One, the Enlightened One, the Morning Glory. And through her journeys to hell and beyond, she has consumed the energy of all in her path—angels, demons, and humans alike. It is said that even Lucifer trembled in her wake. She can make oceans dry up and cities drown. She can make fire rain down from the sky if she is bored. Her reign of punishment and horror ripped open a giant void in the very fabric of mankind, shutting the lord and the sun out from them.

The Lord had hoped those years would soften the people, teach them a lesson, and make them turn back to Him and the heavens. But He had wanted true balance.

And for two thousand years, that's exactly what Aestrangel delivered.

For she is Legion.

Many and all.

And the world will continue to shudder under her rule.

## -PART I-
# THE FALLEN

"*That's why there is forgiveness needed on both sides. I would have never intentionally hurt you. You are my star. My Aestra. You are so special to me, like a daughter. You are unlike any other angel.*"

—CAMAEL

# THE RECAP

Power swirls around me. Consumes me. Infiltrates every fiber of my essence. Darkness swells up with a raucous rush then subsides like calming waves returning to the sea. It leaves me giddy—tickled with the newness and oldness of the feelings all at once. For I am old. And I am new. And I am flame and fire, wave and sea all at once. And I am dancer and dreamer and air and spirit and nothingness and allness and everything and anything. I am Aestrangel, and there is much that dwells inside of me—much that wrestles with the obligations of my own desires and the directions of the one I serve, and the sprinkles of angelic essence that once ruled this body of mine. I can still hear it deep inside. It still talks to me, whispers my name, and tells me secrets of the cosmos. I know the voice so clearly in my soul; a piece of Camael haunts me from within, but I try to ignore it, try to push it away.

With the roll of my head, I shrink down to almost nothing. My form collapses in on itself and spreads out wide along the whisper of a breeze. A sharp buzz echoes throughout each of my descending particles like a swarm of yellow jackets taking flight. I sprinkle myself like a white dusty snow atop the hard-packed earth. Gradually, each moldy flake of me squirms beneath the soil, and I am absorbed into the dirt like thousands of pinpricks piercing my molecules. The earth sings. She whistles as she grows and hums at the prospect of the new life about to sprout up from the depths of her fertile womb. But I am spore, and I take hold of the green buds nestled deep inside her belly, gripping to the sides of them, working my way into their tiny insides, squeezing the life from them, and casting shadows into their hearts. The Earth cries, unable to stop my attack. She moans and shudders and shakes, trying to rid me of her den, trying to force me out of her abode. I have violated her safe space, and she weeps, for she knows her infected children will fester and rot and multiply and spread my disease to the multitudes of people. With the crops infected, the people will suffer for years and years to come. I wonder what it must be like, to be a haven for a child—to harbor a life inside of you. How does she feel knowing I have singlehandedly destroyed her precious progeny? I laugh back at the Earth because her wails are useless. It will take years before the people realize what I have done and decades for them to undo the damage, and there is nothing she can do to communicate her knowledge of my actions.

Now, I wait for the rains to come and push me back up to the surface. When the sun dries the soil, and the breezes come barreling through the plains, I will re-form and carry myself back to Gehenna.

*It is a great responsibility to be the Commanding General in Lucifer's Army.*

My wings, black as the inky night sky, carry me to the faraway places the Morning Star has commanded. In different shapes and structures, I have unleashed my wrath upon the human race, and each time, I think up new and curious ways to exact my fury. I continue to impress the Dark Lord and raise his expectations. He has tasked me with this sacred mission, and I do my best not to disappoint. And yet, I endeavor to control my power—my great and almighty power that grows exponentially with each passing day. I shield it from them all, and even from myself, for if they had the slightest inkling of the true nature of my capabilities, I fear the Demonic Order would look upon me as a threat. But I am growing, changing, shifting, *becoming.* It has gone beyond the power orbs I learned how to make manifest in my hands. I've taught myself how to see through the cosmos using those little gems. But those are mere trinkets. Malek thought my shape-shifting tricks were fascinating, but I think I scared him a little when I shifted into Cronos and swallowed him whole. I can construct cities with the wave of my hand and destroy whole civilizations with the snap of my fingers. In Asphodel, under the cover of the fog-gloom realm, I have secretly been able to have much practice with my abilities, but the power grows so rapidly, that even I am unaware of the extent of my godhood.

*All will know when the time is right.*

I do not trust the others of the Demonic Order, and they don't trust me either, which is not too hard to understand. I get it. I know why Lucifer keeps a close watch over this heart of mine. I know why Malek's new objective is to be my guide, my keeper, my sometime adviser. For there isn't another Daimon in Lucifer's court who rejected the creator the way I have. Sure, the two hundred before me fell in love with the mortals and turned their backs on the creator's love, but Lucifer—he's the mastermind, the Dark Lord, the Morning Star, the Wicked One. There's much more to his intentions than the lusty desire for the human flesh. Not since Lucifer's descent had an angel rebelled so callously, so violently. Until me. And I have accomplished something no other daimon or angel could have even dreamed to accomplish—I spilled angelic blood ... *in Ilarium*. That alone should give the Dark Lord pause to trust me. I know it would give me pause if I were in his shoes.

And that is why I am held at arm's length and given these seemingly high-ranking tasks of causing destruction and chaos on Earth. Lucifer is planning on provoking the Angelos to mobilize and bring about the Great War. But I am not stupid. Lucifer makes me *think* my actions of spreading disease and pestilence and influencing wars between nations will be the catalyst for our Great War, but I know the truth. All of this was set into motion the moment I killed Camael. What I'm doing now is just a bonus. Icing on the cake. And my little "infect the crops" trick was simply that—a trick. A blip. A nothing. I could have done much worse but chose not to. I cannot give all my secrets away yet because I have committed to the Morning Star's side in the final battle to come with the creator, but beyond that? All bets are off.

And speaking of the Great War, as I wait for the rains, I have much time to ponder and think on things that have happened and have yet to come. The biggest discrepancy I see in the whole motivation behind the war between the Daimones and Angelos is *intentions*. What is the end game here? What are Lucifer's true intentions? To rule? To be Lord of all? To overtake the creator? How could he even if he tried? Surely, there will be a great battle, but for Lucifer to fully overthrow the creator... that would be impossible! He's the creator! The Great Artificer! Architect of the Cosmos! The Alpha and the Omega! He has no beginning and no end. Lucifer is not stupid, nor is he foolish enough to think he could rule in the creator's stead. There can never be a moment in time without the creator, for there is only time because of him. Without the existence of god, there would be no existence of the Morning Star. So, what is the goal? *The destruction of everything?*

One thing is for sure, Lucifer desired revenge on Camael. It was Camael's blundering that caused the damnation of Lilith, Lucifer's one true love, and for that, Lucifer had never forgiven him. It was Camael's recommendation for my Calling, Jake, to be denied Ishim, and for that, Lucifer knew *I* would never forgive Camael. I was the key to Lucifer's revenge. My access to Ilarium, and my soul with its angelic design, tainted with humanity and splashed with demonic undertones, was the passageway by which the Morning Star was able to exact his revenge. The death of Camael was set into motion eons ago by Lucifer; it was a matter of time before he could enact it. He used me and his own son Malek to manipulate and fulfill what he himself could not carry out.

And what of Malek? Pure, evil, faithful Malek. Malek with the jet-black hair and stormy eyes in his dashing human form. Malek with his crooked horns and twisted claws in his true shape. Malek who was the Tempter, the Brother, the Teacher, the Redeemer. His poor demonic soul shattered when he learned that he too was merely a pawn in his father's game. His name means king, and as a First Order Daimon, he once had expectations of being seated at the right side of his father, only to be passed over for me—his original Calling. After my black coronation as General, Lucifer made sweeping promises to his disappointed son. He proclaimed that Malek would be a god that the humans would worship and pray to. He would be *Moloch*, in their tongue, and they would offer prayers of protection and safety for their children. And if they did not worship him, Malek would have the power to steal the souls of their firstborns, usher them to Gehenna, and offer them to Lilith's canopy of dead children. *Moloch the Child Eater. Moloch the Soul Devourer. Moloch the Devil.* It all sounded wonderful and deliciously twisted, but Malek was not impressed and subsequently declined his father's offers of godhood. He had had other plans and other visions and had charted a different course for himself. He hadn't anticipated that my darkness would have eclipsed his own.

And for what it's worth, Malek didn't deserve that, much like I didn't deserve the betrayal from my creator, the one I called Father. We were both used and discarded by our respective parental figures, and there is more than a kinship between us. He has grown on me ... more than I care to admit. I have relied on him ... more than I have wanted to. And I trusted him ... more than I probably should. Now the question remains in the hour of darkness when I dethrone the current regime, do I take Malek with me, or do I leave him to the same fate as his father? I guess only time will tell. I guess I will leave that decision to him. No one knows what the soul is truly made up of until they are set against a time of suffering and strife. For all of Lucifer's betrayals, Malek might act on his father's behalf and turn against me. Or he may join my ranks and plot to overthrow me in the future. Violence begets violence in a never-ending cycle. But I'm getting way ahead of myself. And besides, I can smell the musty scent of impending rain. I have work to do.

The skies open, and I am drenched in thousands of places. Each singular raindrop seeps into the earth and pulls each speck of me into its watery dome. From there, I slowly but surely connect with the other droplets to coagulate into a small pool. My thousands of particles rise to the surface of the now muddied field, and I reconnect, reconfiguring myself to some semblance of a form. As a lizard, I dart my tongue and bob my head and adjust to the corporeal design. It makes my mind swim to have been thousands of spores recombined to this cold-blooded shape. I propel myself forward with my small spindly tail and take to the sky as a crow, hawk, eagle, albatross before I envelope myself in my darkness and my black wings take shape and I am whole again. I am Aestrangel, and I will myself back to the self I am most comfortable in. The shape of Aestrangel—not quite angel, not quite demon. She who walks the line between Heaven and Hell. Between Ilarium and Gehenna. Between life and death.

As I race along the night sky on my way back to the depths of Gehenna, I look up to the heavens and sigh. Once, I swelled with pride at the thought of my angelic nature. I served god and god alone. I loved his creations fiercely and unconditionally. I remember longing to have a dream so Camael would put me in the body of a human girl and send me on a mission to help one of the lord's most divine creations. It was all I wanted. All I desired. All I lived for. Until I realized it was all a damned lie. It was all a trick and all for nothing. My existence was a sham, and the creator didn't care about me or my well-being at all. For a brief moment, a vacancy flutters in my heart at the thought of Ilarium and the old life I lived.

Nothing above that sky awaits me. In fact, everything above that sky is probably plotting my demise right about now. A shooting star streaks through the nighttime clouds. Just one. One lone angel dispatched to Earth below to set their special Calling on the straight and narrow. Could it be Revalia, my old friend and companion? Could it be Lozhure, her dedicated lover? I can't tell anymore. The signatures of their streaks are lost to me. In the past, each angel had their own unique display as they were sent careening down to Earth. Now, I view them with my new demonic eyes, and to me, it's barely a flash of light. Uneventful. Dull. Unimportant. In the past, the light show would dazzle and amaze me as one by one the angels would disengage from the light source and boldly race across the sky. But not now. Now, there's only one. A sad one. An uneventful one. An unimportant one. Is it because the angels have far more important things to worry about? Is it because they are concentrated on more pressing matters? Like the Great War to come? Like *me*?

Oh yes, I did do a number on them, didn't I? I surmise they needed to shift their focus from the petty human race for a moment so they could figure out how to deal with me. I'm sure all my chaotic machinations haven't helped much either—I rather did have fun creating those wild earthquakes and bringing the Plague back for a bit was a classic distraction. But through all that, I have to say there is one event I wish I could have witnessed...

*...the aftermath of Camael's death.*

I could only imagine the scene of great wailing and lamentation that must have followed shortly thereafter. The Angelos having to feel pain, strife, and loss and suffering in their astral gene for the first time ever... it would have been glorious to see! I bet it was like being born. Like seeing something for the first time, like when I looked into the heart of the creator and saw that his monstrous visage was not as far off from the creatures that dwelled in Asphodel. And when they realized Camael was gone— lights out—the pain must have resonated so deeply in their souls that it will never be able to be washed away. All of them. The entire Heavenly Host, creator included. And to think—I did that. I caused that pain and suffering. I opened the floodgates of their strife. I wish I could have seen the horrific colors of their sad angel wings.

Bring the Great War. Bring it to the shores of the Earth, to the edges of the cosmos, to the window of The Observatory, to the gates of Gehenna. I fear none. I have been storing all my energy and power for a chance to unleash my rage again because, ultimately, destroying Camael did something to me. It changed me forever. No longer do I err on the side of maybes and what-ifs. No longer do I contemplate the possible outcomes of women burning in cars or men stealing wallets on subways. There are only two objectives in clear sight: win the War on the side of the Morning Star for what the creator has done to me and destroy the Morning Star for what *he* did to me. There can be nothing else and no other way.

For I am Aestrangel—formed from the rarest stardust, shaped in the creator's image, given free will in an angelic cage, commissioned to do the Morning Star's bidding.

I am Aestrangel. All and nothing. Many and none.

I am Aestrangel. Failure is not an option.

CHAPTER TWO

## THE PROPOSAL

T he trip back to Gehenna is swift and hazy. Traversing back and forth through the dark vortex always leaves me feeling a little unsteady and off-kilter, and I seem to briefly lose my sense of where and when. One time on my return, I even lost sense of "who," which was particularly unnerving. But Malek had been waiting for me at the gates that time, and one look of his monstrous smile set me straight.

As soon as I set foot on the rocky terrain of the caverns and get my bearings, my acute senses immediately pick up on an odd hush that has blanketed throughout the gloomy cavity. The caves are quiet. Low-murmured whispers echo in the distance, and the wails of moans and lamentations from the tortured souls in the alcoves are subdued and lulled. Something has shifted. Changed. Like something inhaled deeply and is holding its breath ... waiting. I don't like it. I don't like the feeling of icy anticipation creeping its way through the tips of my feathers. Something inside me says to go directly to the throne room.

The air in the grotto is heavy and thick, and it presses sharply on my chest like a weight. I glide swiftly through the tunnels, trying to avoid making eye contact with the creatures who hang upside down from the craggy ceilings or who are chained to the walls in the niches, but I know they stare at me. I know their eyes are trained on my every movement as I float past them. Each one stops its bellows and groans as it watches me go by. Their one-by-one silencing resonates in the cave. But I keep my head down, daring to not look up, daring to not be met with their faceless expressions and pleading eyes. My focus remains on the stony ground—stained dark brown with old blood, while pools of bright-red new blood coagulate between the cracks of the rocks. The blood pools sing in my head. It's a familiar song, like the one Mother Earth sang to me when I penetrated her with my virus. The blood pools cry out like they too anticipate something about to happen— an agonizing torment, a guttural scream like the blood is still being released from its life source. The song hums in my ears, and I move faster through the cave. My wings arch slightly forward and propel me with a swift motion.

The feeling in the throne room is no different. When I enter, time seems to stop, gasping at my arrival. The Dark Lord sits regally in his chair, surrounded by figures whispering in low voices, but at my arrival, the huddle dissipates, and all eyes shift to my direction. Have I intruded on a secret meeting? Should I not be here? Lilith, Malek, and a creature I am not familiar with spread out so that I can see Lucifer clearly.

Lilith is the first to move from their semi-circle. Her long shadowy hair slides along the floor, and she slithers

her thick snaky body to her corner of the room back to her black canopied bed. The weight of her snake tail pushes down on the white bones of her dead children adorning the bottom portion of the bed. That is her punishment for rejecting Adam, the first man—for every live birth she has, she must suffer one hundred dead children thereafter. Cursed to live an eternity of fertility, gestation, birth, and loss because she enacted her God-given free will and decided not to be subservient to Adam. Falling in love with Lucifer in the form of Samael didn't help her cause with the creator too much either. But again, how loving and just was her sentence? Where was the forgiveness there? The bones crunch with a hideous sound, and she winces for a split second before she props into position and exhales. The bone crunch reminds her, yet again, of her never-ending torment, of the never-ending wailing in her mother's heart—like the Earth, like the blood. I look to her with a pained expression, for there is real sadness in my heart for the injustice exacted upon her, but her black eyes only shoot back contempt.

I pull away from her gaze when the Morning Star outstretches his arms to me. "Aestrangel, my love, you've returned!" A smile spreads across his face, but I hesitate. I am still outside the reach of his silver aura, and my senses are still in my complete control. I know the moment I enter his magnetic field that I will be subject to his charms and sweet melodies. I'd rather keep my distance for now until I've figured out what is going on. He leans forward in his chair, summoning me to come closer to him, but I stay flat-footed in my place. The corners of his mouth descend a little, and for a split second, a flash of lightning streaks across his dark eyes. But I remain where I stand, and he recoils his extended arm and sits back against his ebony throne. "You hear the echoes, Aestrangel? The voices of the damned? It's because of you, Morning Glory." He closes his eyes and inhales, breathing in the sounds of the tortured souls from beyond Gehenna's walls.

"It succeeded then?" I ask, but I know full well the extent of my disease.

"And then some," he states with pride.

Malek is at Lucifer's right. I look at him, and there is nothing less than an expression of bewilderment on his face. His stormy eyes are raining something awful, and he shifts nervously from one foot to the next. He stands before me in the shape that is a mixture of his demonic self, and his human self—the familiar and the grotesque. From the waist up, he is man—handsome and dashing, the brother who swept me off my feet in Arizona. From the waist down, he is demon—stony legs and gnarled claws, the monster who scared me in Brooklyn. A wave of worry creeps its way into my heart for I have always known Malek to be the calm, the collected, the cocky, and the confident. But right now, he's merely a shell. Defeated. Malek, but not. In my mind's eye, I try to reach him, try to scream to him, "What's wrong?" When he hears me (because I know he does), he quickly widens his eyes and drops his gaze to his cloven feet.

I instinctively take a step closer and try to make sense of the hooded creature at Lucifer's left. The Morning Star is keen to notice my curiosity, and he raises his eyebrows. "Ahh," he coos, "you haven't been introduced yet, have you?"

Dumbly, I shake my head.

He extends his arm to me once again for a proper introduction, and hypnotically, I take another step toward them. "This is Alukah. My daughter. Lilith's daughter. Malek's sister."

"His *true* sister," Lilith hisses from her bed, an obvious dig at the deceptive storyline Malek and I had played out on Earth not so long ago.

His metallic aura pulsates stronger. "Alukah, Aestrangel," he says as he gestures his head from her to me.

Alukah pulls back the hood that covered her face and bows her head to me. I hear a faint giggling from the figure, and when she raises her head, I can't quite make out the structure of her visage. I rapidly blink my eyes in hopes of clearing them from any kind of grit or fog, but no, as I squint and shift my focus, I see that Alukah doesn't have a face! Not a real one at least. I step closer, one more foot, to get a better view. There are eyes in a fixed position, and fangs descended from where a mouth should be, but her face... her wretched and hideous face is in constant motion. Ever shifting and changing like a kaleidoscope or a hologram. I can't help but stare, trying to focus my eyes and catch the image of her true self, her true face. But this is her true face! And the more I stare, the more I see three distinct personas, three distinct entities at war within her and with each other—each fighting to come through, each struggling for dominance over her demonic body. There are flashes of beauty and serenity when the expressions change over, but for the most part, there is not much more than darkness and horror.

*And that is beautiful, too...*

At first, I freeze from the strangeness of it all. A piercing panic shudders throughout my body and my black wings pulse a deep raven purple, but she is mesmerizing— revolting and lovely wrapped in one. I breathe her in and relax my body on the exhale.

Alukah clasps her hands together. "The dark has come. We shall begin!" she says excitedly. Her voice grates on my ears like seashells crunching up on the sandy shore. Like jagged stones violently rubbing together.

"Patience, daughter. Soon enough," Lucifer assures. "Come, Aestrangel," he motions for me to sit next to him in *my* chair.

I obey his command but am still wary of the scenario. "Tell me, O Dark One," I say with a side smile, "what is the meaning of this ominous reception?"

He smiles back at me, and with a flick of his finger, a silver light encircles my head and melts down over my face. I am washed in his aura, bathed in his astral kiss. I am warm and comforted and safe in his domain. "Hardly ominous, wouldn't you say?" he says, sending another kiss to me.

This one goes straight to my stomach, and I quiver from the pleasurable tickle that extends itself down my legs. "Certainly not," I say, relaxing in my chair. From the corner of my eye, I see Malek turn his head away.

Alukah jumps up and down like a little child. "Oh please, Father! Please!" she begs, but Lucifer raises his hand in front of her, and she is silenced, recoiling like a beaten animal.

Another astral kiss penetrates me deeply. My wings wrap around to the front of my body, and I tightly grip the arms of my throne. My feathers strobe their colors in a frenzy as the Morning Star's aura creeps into every crevice of my essence. It pulls me up, raises me from the seat, lifts me to a crescendo, and holds me there in a euphoric wave before I swell up with a surge of warmth and ecstasy.

"Reward for a job well done?" I ask breathlessly, easing against the back of the soft velvet throne. A thin sheen of sweat has formed on my forehead, and I wipe it away with the tips of my wing.

"Of sorts," he replies with a chuckle. "I have another request of you."

"Another mission?"

"Of sorts," he repeats, but this time there's a subtle change in his tone. A change so slight that even the keenest of ears would not have picked up on it, but I did. I sit straight up at attention.

Lucifer notices my uneasiness. "Certain developments have been brought to my attention. Developments that could give us a clear advantage in the Great War to come," he says calmly. "But there's only one way that we can be sure of its validity."

Alukah's fingers start to twitch with anticipation. Her kaleidoscope face rapidly goes in and out of focus, and she becomes nothing more than a blur. But I can see she is smiling, her fangs long and quite visible.

"What does this have to do with me?" I ask, but when I do, I direct my question to Malek, who has been eerily quiet this whole time. He says nothing. There is no response from him. The look on his face is disconcerting. So much that I feel the fear again making its way back into my mind.

"My Alukah," Lucifer begins. "She is my prophetess. My vampiress. My seer. Maiden, Mother, Crone in one. She can tell me things of the future and of the past. But her devilish ways require a simple sacrifice."

I freeze.

"A suckle of your honey, my busy bee."

I furrow my brow. "Excuse me?"

"A few drops of your essence, your angelic blood if you will. Then Alukah can tell me true if the stories I am hearing are correct."

Alukah strides over to my side, sweeps my hair over my shoulder, and exposes my neck. "A little prick, one and two. A little taste to tell me true," she says with her raspy voice then leans forward and presses her teeth to my flesh.

Her whole body shakes as she takes in my essence, my life force, my angelic blood. I surmise she's never tasted someone as sweet as me before—for all my darkness, hints of angel light still run in my veins. I start to swoon as she transfers images to my astral mind. I see her birth: she climbs out of a snake pit with a thousand puncture marks and climbs into Lilith's arms. Lilith suckles the venom from Alukah's wounds, and as Alukah hungrily feeds from Lilith's breast, her fangs descend, tearing off her mother's nipple. I see her playing in Asphodel: she dances with the fog monsters and bites at their ankles, draining them of life. She had a face then. Beautiful, like her mother. Stormy, like her father. I see her playing with a young Malek, and she bites him too. She absorbs much of his power and energy and nearly leaves him for dead until Lucifer comes to reprimand her. It takes Malek a long time to recover. So long that the Maiden, Mother, and Crone splintered within Alukah and stole her face.

Malek comes up from behind her and swings Alukah away from my neck. She slides across the stone floor as Lucifer rushes over to her side.

I look up at Malek, and he nods. From the visions she showed me, I know he was saving me from what had happened to him. I nod back in thanks.

"Speak, Daughter!" Lucifer commands.

Alukah writhes on the floor, moaning. "'There are four things that never say 'enough.' The grave, the barren womb, land that is not satisfied with water, and fire...'"

I know those words. She quotes the sacred text of the humans. The Book of Proverbs.

"She speaks the prophecy," Malek whispers to me, but still, I am confused.

"I... I don't understand..." I mumble.

"You will create a weapon for him," he continues. "He believes this is something only you can do."

"What? What are you talking about?" my voice rises, and I quickly stop talking when Lucifer's eyes dart in my direction.

"'... and under a female servant who replaces her mistress...'"

I tug on Malek's arm, forcing his ear to my mouth. "Me? Is she saying I'm a female servant?" I whisper frantically.

"Can it be done, Alukah?" Lucifer asks for confirmation.

"It can. It shall."

The Morning Star helps his daughter back up to her feet, and she shrouds her face with her hood once again. He turns on his heel and faces me. "It is so," he says.

"What is?" I ask.

Lucifer breathes in deep and begins. "You shed angelic blood in Ilarium, Aestrangel. The murder of Camael ultimately changed the landscape of the heavens. It was brutal. And visceral. And oh, so wonderful." He smiles.

I can't help but return the smile at the memory.

"And with this change," he continues, "certain *openings* were left in its wake. The World Window in The Observatory was cracked. The Demonic Order has determined that the crack is wide enough for one of us to get through. Someone small. A child."

"A shapeshifter," Malek pleads, but Lucifer raises a hand toward him, silencing him like he silenced Alukah.

"A pure," Alukah croaks.

"We need a child born to do this. They can travel the vortex and penetrate the crack. Once inside Ilarium, our infection will spread, and the Great War will be but a whimper for the Angelos. Time is of the essence, and..."

This time I lift *my* hand to silence *him.* He stops, surprised at my arrogant command. "So, you're saying one of us. A child. But they would be detected the moment they tried to access the upper vortex and..."

I stop.

I pause.

Lucifer's face darkens in disappointment. He's disappointed that I hadn't figured it out. That it should have been so very clear to me because I'm crafty and clever and smart and powerful and all-knowing and...

I stare at him hard, disgusted at the suggestion of being his broodmare. Lilith chuckles to herself in her corner, and my rage flares.

"The scent of Ilarium is still fresh in you. There's enough of it to mask detection," Lucifer says, and this time, his voice takes somewhat of a pleading tone. "There is still something boldly holy about you. Something that could easily pass on and slip through that crack. I wouldn't ask this of you if I didn't think it was necessary or important or worthy."

I say nothing.

Cold hatred rips me from the inside.

"Lilith would do it herself, but..."

I continue to stare.

"Think on it, and..."

I whip my head around to Malek. "Will it be you? Is this your plan?" I spit.

He shakes his head, and his diamond-shaped medallion bounces off his chest. His eyes plead with mine in a painful exchange. "No, Aestrangel, I..." he stammers.

"Think on it," Lucifer repeats. "The creator chose a human to usher in the Redeemer. A human with flaws, disadvantages, and mortality. I can't think of a better, more suited mother than you—someone to usher in The Conqueror, someone who has walked all avenues of life as angel, and human, and demon, and somewhere in between. What better role model for the One Who Will Destroy the Angelos than the strange angel herself?"

## CHAPTER THREE

# THE PLAN

*S**trange angel.*

Lucifer's words cut me deep. He purposefully called me that to invoke a certain feeling in me, and I fell right into his hand. Strange angel. That was the moniker given to me by my human Calling, Jake Parker, all those years ago. To hear his words, to recall his face and remember his scent and his touch and... it's maddening. The love and desire I felt for him sicken me; it consumes my core with a corrosive stench. And even though it was a brief blissful moment with a lifetime of consequence, I needed that moment in time to become what I am now. I needed Jake Parker to be the catalyst for my awakening, and for that particular gift he has given me, I will be eternally indebted.

But Jake is mine. His memory, his essence, his teachings... they are mine and mine alone to do with as I please. How dare Lucifer bring him up! After everything I've gone through! Lucifer's reference to Jake is deliberate and calculated, and the rage within me rushes to the surface with a surging heat. If I unleash it now, I will take down this throne room, and everything in it, in a colossal firestorm. I jump up from my seat. My wings crack open behind me—a mass of charred feathers with red flamed tips poised and ready to attack at my mental command. A slight gasp sucks in through Alukah's fangs, and the sound of it snaps me into a temporary calm. I still must remain as reserved as possible.

"You object. That's understandable," Lucifer says. "Take all the time you need, my dear. I know this is a heavy task I ask of you. But do this for me, and you will be greatly rewarded."

I step down from the stony stage and retract my wings. "I need to think," I say and walk down the main corridor that leads to the Hall of Pleasure.

No sooner do I reach the edge of the tunnel than Malek is right behind me, hand on my shoulder, taking deep gulping breaths. I spin around to meet his gaze. "What?" I bark.

"Aestrangel, I..."

"Didn't know? Didn't have a hand in this? Didn't help devise this almighty plan?"

He reaches for my hands, and I sigh. I know he had nothing to do with this. The expression on his face had told me that. And Malek has never done or said anything to maliciously hurt me. I have no cause to think he would ever have a hand in his father's schemes.

"After all we've been through together?" he asks.

I nod weakly. "I know. I know," I relent.

He holds my hands together in his and raises them to his soft lips. He showers my fingers with hundreds of gentle peck-like kisses, and I can't help but smile at him. His gray eyes swirl a lovely pasture scene with woodland creatures drinking peacefully at a babbling brook. I know he shows me this scene to help calm me down, and I must admit, it works. Malek always knows how to settle my soul, and for a moment, I am distracted by the forest and forget about the Morning Star's mission to breed me. I feel safe with Malek. Content. He makes me feel... I don't know ... *complete.*

"It's always been you," I say before I realize the words have left my lips.

He narrows his eyes quizzically. "How so?"

My shoulders tense up. I'm a little surprised that I spoke my thoughts out loud, and a little surprised by his reaction. "Well, you told me when we were on that Wild West Adventure that it was all about me—the things you did, the mission we were on. But really, I think it's been about you. About how you make me feel. And how I know you're always at my back with my best interest..."

He releases my hands and takes a step back. "Wait," he protests, "are you saying..."

My mouth twists slightly at the corner. "Aren't *you* saying? Haven't you already said?"

"Love you?" he exclaims, his mouth gaping wide in a surprised expression.

To hear him say the words strikes a nerve in me—a hopeful jolt that is like an electric pulse in my veins. But he pauses, steps back yet again, and my head cocks to the side in newfound confusion. "But I..." I stammer like an idiot thrown off guard.

"Feel a kinship, yes. Empathy? To a degree, yes. But I am pure demon, Aestrangel. Have you forgotten? Love is not a word in my vocabulary."

The tone of his voice raises my curiosity. There's a hint of a lie in his truth and a hint of truth in his lie. But even though I don't fully believe him, like a balloon letting out air, I am deflated. I thought about everything that we have been through, through all our missions, the closeness that he and I had achieved had transcended beyond. I don't know. Do I love him? I don't know what it is that I feel. It's not the hot passion flame that had been sparked for Jake Parker. But it's more than kinship. For all my almighty power, for all my dominion over lesser beings, for my status of wrathful daimon who shall destroy all with a mere flick of the wrist, I feel like a defeated mortal wanting to curl up in a corner and cry myself to sleep.

"Don't mistake feelings of a common denominator for love. Just because we have been together in dark times and in good times…"

"Stop. Forget it," I say dismissively and turn my back from him.

His hand clasps my shoulder, and he turns me back around, glaring hard at me with his steel gray eyes. There are storm clouds circling into violent tornadoes, and I get lost in them, hypnotized, as if I could float away in the maelstrom and never be seen again. "Answer me this," he says. "Do *you* love *me*?"

*A demon is all-knowing,* a voice inside my mind chimes. Camael's voice punches through, but I shush him away.

My reflection stares back at me against the dark gray sky of Malek's eyes, and I want to scream. How pathetic I look. How pathetic I feel. Like a weepy, stupid human girl mourning over her unrequited love. *Dumb. Dumb. Dumb. Dumb…* "I don't know what I feel," I snap, coming back to reality.

"Having been a human damaged your psyche, didn't it?" he tries to explain.

"Tainted, not damaged," I correct, and Camael's voice flutters like echoes in my mind again. "I can think quite clearly, thank you very much." I start to turn again, but he stops me, again.

"Look, I didn't mean to..."

"Just let me go, Malek. I really have a lot on my mind and..."

"I don't want that for you. I don't. The thought of you being with someone else, some*thing* else, enrages me. And it enrages me even more that I can't do anything to stop it."

"He says I have a choice," I tease.

Malek raises his eyebrows, and I chuckle. But not really, because it's not funny. He and I both know that there is no choice in this matter. Lucifer sets up the terms and the guidelines and presents the material with his subjects getting to truly believe that they have a say in their ultimate fate. Malek and I both know this is not the case with the Father of Lies. My fate in this matter has already been spelled out.

"You've been different since I came back here," I say. "You've been different to me ever since your father crowned me with black thorns and made me his General."

"You've been different since you murdered Camael," he shoots back.

He's right. We're both right. Both our worlds are changing and spinning at such a rapid pace that it's sometimes hard to catch on to something tangible. I thought Malek was my anchor to hold on to, but I guess I was wrong. "Didn't think I had it in me, did ya?" I say playfully.

"Oh no. I knew you did," he says with a hint of pride. "It just seemed to happen so..."

"Abruptly?"

"Yes. Abruptly. Regardless of all that. All I know is this: I don't want you getting hurt. If what happened to my mother is any indication of your future, I am very fearful. Or worse." His voice trails off.

"Got any secret medallions to keep me safe this time around?" I joke.

"Oh no. I think you'll be fine on your own. And I think that's what bothers me too. That a part of me knows you'll be okay. That you don't need me to protect you or guide you anymore. You outgrew me."

"Oh, stop," I say and punch his shoulder playfully, *humanly*, like how we joked around in the corporeal world. "I wouldn't say I outgrew you. I would say more like, I caught up."

"Don't play coy," he scoffs. "I know you're hiding something. I know you too well, Aestrangel."

He smiles wide, his charming and familiar smile, and a part of me melts like a teenage girl on the inside. He pulls my arms and drags me in for an icy embrace, and the essence of his demonic soul envelopes me. I rest my head in the hollow of his shoulder. My lips brush up against the soft skin of his neck, make their way to the lobe of his ear, and whisper, "Something." He pulls back and smirks at me, and I release his hold.

"Walk with me, Aestrangel," Lucifer calls as he emerges from the tunnel. "Let me at least try to explain my thought process."

My face falls. I don't want to leave Malek, but he gives me a slight nod directing me to obey. Malek walks away, and I move closer to the Morning Star, sucked into his magnetic aura. He wraps his arm around my shoulder and pulls me tightly into the crook of his arm like a loving father would do when guiding their child. He pulsates with pure energy—a high voltage of electricity and malevolence.

*<Have you made a choice?>* he asks, his voice not in the caves but in my head.

"Did you send Malek after me?" I respond. A question for a question. I try to maintain some sort of upper hand.

"No," he says out loud, "he does as he pleases. As will you," he adds, circumventing back to his original question.

I chuckle despite myself. I know that *he* knows that *I* know his request isn't really a request at all, and I refuse to play into the subterfuge. Lucifer is truly no better than the creator in that respect.

"Will it be you?" I ask, inquiring about the potential father for my eventual offspring.

"Oh, I wish it could be," he gushes with a marked sincerity in his voice. "Could you imagine the child that we could produce? He would mount the world and breathe fire and leave nothing in the cosmos but a gaping void. He would reduce time and space to nothing and erase the entire astral plane! But sadly, I am not for you. I am devoted to one soul and one soul alone. My Lilith!" He sighs when he breathes her name. "My snake dancer. My seaside serpent from the Land of Nod."

*So, demons* can *love...*

He leads me down to one of the alcoves in the rocky hall. There, a man hangs suspended with chains from the ceiling. The chains are hooked into the flesh of his back, and his skin is stretched thin and high above him. Beneath him, a demon in the form of a goat jabs its horns into the man's stomach, puncturing the flesh, and tearing him open inch by inch. Every time the horns slice deeper, the man howls in agony.

"Watch him," Lucifer commands and points to the man. "Watch how he writhes when Azazel carves into him. Does he look like he is in true pain? Or is there something more?"

I shake my head. "No. He enjoys it."

"When his belly is torn open and his insides spill to the floor, what do you think he will feel then?"

"Pleasure," I say confidently.

"And when Azazel feasts on the entrails? What of the man's condition then?"

I stare at the goat, at his bloodied horns, and the man swinging in his bindings crying out with agonizing shrieks. The scene becomes clear to me as the horn shreds another section of flesh from his body. "Ecstasy."

"Exactly. These are the torments of the truly wicked— of the human souls who have no place in Ilarium. They are not sorry for the atrocities they committed in their human form and have set to live out eternity in constant torture. Before me, their poor souls were set to wander the Earth aimlessly—neither here, nor there—lost and alone. I provided a space for them. A place where they could live out their darkest fantasies."

"What made this one so wicked?" I ask as I gesture to the hanging man.

"That one killed his whole family. He forced his own father to watch as he murdered his mother and siblings before he took his own life. Acts like that don't go unnoticed, especially by me. And when it was revealed there was a true vacancy in his heart, I knew I would have some room for him. He was the exception to the rule because I would not have classified him as *truly* wicked, but he was close enough. A true family man."

*So, he does play fast and loose with his rules.*

"And really, at the end of the day, isn't it all about family?"

There he goes again, trying to insert his twisted sense of *family* into the conversation. Maybe he hopes to awaken my maternal instincts.

"You'll see when you have a child of your own. I am proud of all of mine, albeit disappointed at the same time. See, my children, while they are devoted to me, their father, they are also bound by their demonic nature. And while they live to serve me, I know that is both a blessing and a curse. They would not do for me what the Redeemer did for the creator, and that is because I give all my children free will. True free will. Not some spokes with eyes on a giant wheel."

One thing Camael did teach me well was that Lucifer was the Father of Lies, but there's something in the way the Morning Star speaks that leads me to think that he truly believes the words that come out of his mouth. It's almost sad, in a way, to believe in your own lies so adamantly, so fervently, that they start to become real.

"When he created his son, he got it all wrong," he continues. "But nonetheless, the man was a great prophet, a loving son, and a Great Teacher. Contrary to popular belief, I have much respect and admiration for my brother, even if he reeked with mortality. After his death, he came here to Gehenna and stayed with me for three days. I'd be lying if I said I wasn't curious about him—to see what made him tick, so to speak. We were supposed to make a deal, you know. I released to him a number of souls, who had since begged forgiveness, with the understanding that the Creator would give to me something so special and so valuable in return. He never held up his end of the bargain, and before I could act, the Great Teacher was back to finish up his Calling on Earth. So again, your creator betrayed me."

"What did you ask for in return?" I say as the hanging man's bowels spill to the floor with an echoing *plop*.

Lucifer, distracted by the display, claps his hands together happily. "Look! Look at how meticulously Azazel wraps the entrails. And when he's done, the wound will close back up, and we can start all over again tomorrow." He's a speck of giddy, like Alukah before she drank from me.

"Riveting," I feign excitement.

Lucifer *tsks* with displeasure, but I don't care. I know he purposefully avoided my question.

"And think of this, Aestrangel. The hypocrisy of the creator shines through yet again! Here I am, my brothers and I, relegated to the depths of the dark because of our love for human women—their progeny forced to work in service to him as Watchers in his grand human/angel design. But, when he got curious and fell in love with the Redeemer's mortal mother, a virgin no less, that's suddenly okay. All is well."

"But, the Redeemer suffered," I say, remembering my old teachings.

"Yes. The creator allowed his own child to suffer and die. The Redeemer succeeded in his Calling, but the price was a hefty one. It was wrong to make a mortal such as that," he sighs in contemplation as he glides away from me. "Even still, all parents want the best for their children. You'll understand soon enough."

"I never said yes."

He pauses and turns. "<But you did,>" he says in the ancient tongue of my ancestors.

And that is that. The book is closed. I will be used as a mating tool to bring forth a child who will in turn be used to destroy the heavens. And all my power and glory can't stop it. Despite the things I've done, the chaos I've caused, the fear I've instilled in the human heart, the lives I've brutally taken—none of that matters, for I am at the mercy of the Morning Star. I am merely a rung on the ladder of the Demonic Order, much like I was once a feather on the wing of the Angelic Order. I am an underling, a servant, a vessel, regardless of my rank or name.

"Malek, then?" I call before he drifts out of sight. Because maybe, just maybe I can salvage something from this experience if I am to be paired with Malek. "Will you send Malek to me?"

"No," he says with the words of the humans this time. "I don't see that happening. There needs to be a union that is perfect and true."

"Why not Malek?" I hopelessly inquire.

"Because. He loves you too much."

# THE BECOMING

Alukah takes me to a place deep inside the bowels of Gehenna called the Black Keep. It is beyond Asphodel, beyond the Hall of Punishment, beyond the Morning Star's throne room, even beyond the walls of Erebos—the place of ungodly suffering where Lucifer's most wicked minions reserve their torments for the supremely vile. The Black Keep is nothing more than a cell, a cage with no windows to peak out of and a large iron cast door. I'm not sure what this place is used for as there are no signs of recent physical activity. But the remoteness of it, the way it is set off from every other nook and cranny in this dark domain gives me a familiar feeling about it. It reminds me a lot like The Observatory in Ilarium, except it's somewhat the opposite, the very antithesis of what The Observatory was made for. The Observatory was meant as a hub station—a summit of power where angels were sent on their way to their Callings. The room was meant for a single purpose—observing! But the Black Keep is the reverse—it is a place of true isolation, away from even the sweetest of punishments from the harpy-like beasts. It makes sense that Lucifer would design a place such as this in his abode. In fact, everything about Gehenna darkly mirrors Ilarium—the similarities between the two domains are uncanny because Lucifer's design was taken from his prior knowledge. Ilarium was his home, and he fashioned his own territory based on that perfect design. It was all he knew, but he twisted and turned it to suit his dark needs and desires.

Contrary to the congregational feel of The Observatory, the Black Keep is a silent space where there is nothing. A great absence. It chills me to think this is where he intends for me to breed.

"Time is soon. Time is near," Alukah growls with her sandpaper voice. "Maiden, Mother, Crone is here."

I don't bother to look at her. I'm much too interested in the chains dangling from the walls.

She sees me eyeing the potential weapon and pulls down her black hood revealing her abnormal face. "You must not fight. You must not get ideas. You will bear the child despite all your tears."

Still, I refuse to respond.

"If so, I'll be back again. And my tricks, my tricks, my punishment, and such…"

"Enough," I interrupt her sing-song words of foreboding. "Enough. Let's just get this over with."

Her hologram shifty face pauses at a demon-clown smile for a second before rotating back to her kaleidoscope visage. I think she tries to frighten me, but when she sees I am unfazed by her unsettling expression, she walks out the iron door, slamming it behind her. She claps her hands together and giggles until I can no longer hear her.

I exhale furiously and sit down on the stone bench against the wall, but it's not a bench, not really. It's more of a rudimentary bed for me to breed with a demon, and it's quite possibly the place where Lucifer intends for me to give birth to whatever distinguished creature he expects me to bear. Without realizing it consciously, my black wings have wrapped themselves around my back protectively, comfortingly. I'm just a cog in his wheel, a spoke in his ever-turning plot. And when this is all over, I will have a plot of my own. This is not finished. Not by a long shot.

Alukah doesn't scare me. This place doesn't scare me. It's not fear in the silence of this tomb, but more like heightened anticipation. Disgust. I do not want this. I am angel. I am demon. I was not meant to be a creator of sorts. This I know in my dark soul of dark souls. I close my eyes and let the silence of the Black Keep wash over and through me. I let the soundless pressure fill my chest and rise with every breath. I remember a time when I would reach out to the creator for love and guidance, for help and some sort of sign to push me in the right direction. I remember when he would answer my pleas with his musical voice, and it warmed me with a sense of purpose and light. Now I have found my own voice, one that speaks clearly and true with no musical qualities or false pleasantries. My voice tells me to be strong, to persevere, and to be true to myself regardless of what my ultimate goals may be.

*My voice tells me to be not afraid...*

A loud, clamoring din breaks into my thoughts like jangling hooks scraping against the rocky floor. My aura shifts, and immediately, my wings crack out behind me as

I stand up at attention. The noise grows louder, gets closer, and my senses tell me the approaching figure is massive. I ready myself for the worst—plant my feet in a defensive stance and fold my arms across my chest.

"Breathe," I say to myself, "just breathe."

The iron door swings open, and a beast enters the room dragging a scythe behind him. He is massive, giant-like with skin made of some kind of combination of leather and stone. Rust-colored spikes protrude from his arms and chest, and his face is covered with a metal helm, but his eyes glow yellow from behind the mask. He is a warrior's nightmare, a demon of punishment, one of the fiercest in Lucifer's Army. When he breathes, smoky air dances around him and permeates the room. My stomach turns to think that Lucifer would even think to send this, this, *thing* to be with me.

I stay in my position, my wings completely fanned out and pulsing from purple to black to blue to silver and back to black partially to distract him and partially to give him a warning to stay clear of me. "Stay back, demon!" I hiss at him, but he merely chuckles a deep, rolling sound from his belly and moves closer to me.

The spikes from his body ooze a foul-smelling liquid. The tips of each needle expand open, and the substance trickles out. I know he means to penetrate me with them and infect every inch of me with his essence to ensure that a child will be created in any and every demonic way possible. To think about the type of offspring this monster would produce turns my stomach. I would have to be insane to allow this!

"I said to stay back!" I say again, my voice rising.

"I have been commanded to take you," he growls.

I close my eyes and let a rush of energy surge from the bottoms of my astral feet. Waves of blue electricity rise to my fingertips, and I stretch my arms out creating a pulsing force field all around me. He grumbles and pushes closer to me, but a shock from my protective light sends him flying back against the stone wall. He falls to his knees, huffs, and gets back up, advancing toward me yet again in an attempt to grab me, hold me down, lick the side of my face through his blood-stained helm, lie on top of me, puncture my entire body with his spikes, and inject his life force into me.

But I have other plans.

I put my palms close together and in the space between them, I will a black light orb to manifest. In the negative space, I curl the ball in my hand and hurl it at him. The orb lands on his chest between his spikes, and it shocks him with black lightning. He cries out in agony as one by one his spikes fall from his chest and arms leaving gaping holes all over his body. I hover over him as he writhes on the floor, twisting and squirming in a pool of his own blood and pus. Without thinking, I extend my arms out over him, palms faced down, and like magnets, I begin to draw him up and into me. His demonic soul is orange, and it shoots up like tiny twisters from his wounds and into my hands. He tastes metallic and rusty, like sucking on metal coins, but even through the bitterness of it all, I draw him into me, absorb him, drink him in, and take his power and source as my own. I incorporate him into me, infusing myself with a new color and a new strength.

He is now with me.

I am now with him.

His name is Mantus.

And we are *becoming.*

He screams inside my head as I watch his body shrivel down to nothing but a pile of sand. "Peace," I whisper to him on the inside, and his cries slowly subside from a raging roar to nothing more than a mere whimper. How the mighty have fallen. How the mighty have grown!

I wait in the Black Keep, knowing that Lucifer will send another after the first failed attempt. I surmise he's not pleased with the destruction of Mantus, and I know there will be another demon to try to seduce me.

When the next one shows up, I am ready. Bathed with my new abilities, I immediately engage my would-be lover in combat. His skin is red and smooth, and he is stronger, nimbler than Mantus, with the upper torso of a human man, and the lower portion of a furry goat. I warn him to keep away from me, to leave if he knows what is good for him, but he laughs and jumps around on his spring-like legs. He kicks at me with his hooves. I hadn't anticipated this swift movement, and I fall back to the stone bed. His red horns protrude from the sides of his head like two chunks of concrete, and I grab onto them as he pins me down and separates my legs. He tries desperately to penetrate me with the long, thin structure that expands against my thigh and creeps closer to the crevice below my torso. He's like a crazed animal, jutting at me with uncontrollable stabbing motions, trying to insert himself to mate, but I hoist myself up, pushing all my weight down on his horns. I wriggle my wings out from behind me, and with my new orange flash of power, my feathers wrap around us with a fiery embrace and singe the hair and flesh of the lower part of his body. He screams and tries to buck away from me, but my grip on his horns is too strong. With a final, explosive yank, I tear them off from the sides of his skull, spraying the both of us with his dark brown blood. I raise my wings to cover his head and catch the blood, and my feathers are drenched. My orange fire sucks up every last ounce of him, and he whittles down to nothing more than a pile of bones on top of me.

He is now with me.

I am now with him.

His name is Pan.

And we are *becoming*.

I make a pile of Pan's bones and Mantus's sand in the corner of the room as a warning sign for the next one who dares come to me. My body is covered in Pan's dried blood, but my aura screams a new color of brown. I have barely finished erecting my shrine when there is a faint knock on the door. I assume it's another hideous creature attempting to have a shot with the strange angel, or perhaps it's Lucifer himself reprimanding me for obliterating two of his most powerful soldiers, so I ready myself for an argument with the Dark Lord and open the door. But the face that greets me on the other side is not the porcelain visage of the Morning Star, nor the deformed figure of some mangled being. This figure is familiar. This figure is gentle. This figure is that of the one I've known long ago and pined for throughout the ages.

This is the figure of Jake Parker.

And my world completely stops.

My heart flutters. My heart skips. My heart seems to jump out of this pseudo-body of mine, and a fuzzy haze takes root in my head as if I'm drunk or in a dream. I know he isn't real. I know the magics that glamour this demon must be extremely strong and volatile. But I am almost in a trance at the sight of his visage. Spellbound by my memory of what was and what could have been.

*Jake. My Jake. My human love.*

Uncontrollably, my wings flash different tones of pinks, purples, greens, and golds. He smiles at me with his brown eyes, and something stirs inside of me. "Hello, my strange angel," he purrs, and his voice sends me into a tailspin of memory.

"Jake?" I ask, dumbfounded. "Is that really you?" The words come out so carelessly, so mindlessly. I know it's not him. Can't be him. But a deep part of me stirs inside and *wishes* it to be really him.

"Who else would it be?" he counters slowly.

"I... I don't..." I stammer.

He moves into the room and closes the door behind him. A part of me doesn't believe it's truly him, but there is a part of me that doesn't care—a part of me that wants to reach out and smother him with a thousand kisses. It has been so long.

He puts out his arms and grabs my hands in his. "Aestra O'Neill," he says looking me over. "Aestra O'Neill in her true form."

Something like a blush of embarrassment rushes to my cheeks, and I wrap my wings underneath my extended arms to cover my bloodied, naked body. Jake smiles, letting me know he doesn't care. "Do you think that matters to me? C'mon! You remember how I said I always had a hard time figuring you out! You were like this giant mystery to me, and I was determined to figure you out. And after all this time, when I learned the truth about who you really are, about *what* you really are, do you think I was surprised at all?" The cadence of his voice puts me into a swoon of memory. It relaxes me, takes me back to a different time, a different place.

"I guess not," I say sheepishly and relax my wings.

"Let's sit. We have a lot to talk about."

We make our way to the stone bench. He's the same. The same way that I remember him, but not. I close my eyes tightly when he squeezes my hand because one by one I am assaulted by fragments of images—one of his kiss, one of his touch, one of his poetry, one of his wife, one of his dead child, one of his life's work—image after image ravages my brain, makes me swoon, and muddles me in confusion. "I... I watched you *die!*" I yell when I've figured out the chain of events. "They put me in The Observatory, and I watched you from above. I watched your whole life play out—your wife, your kids, your teaching job. And I watched you die! You're gone. Lights out. I... I..." Memories of his death start to flood in. Memories of Jake not being permitted into the rank of Ishim. Memories of me renouncing the creator. Memories of my pact with Lucifer. Memories of slaughtering Jake's entire bloodline. "I went through time and space to eliminate you ... to *erase* you!" I pull back from his grip and rub the sides of my temples hoping to rub some type of understanding into my consciousness.

"Oh Aestra," he says, "I know all the lengths you've gone through, but you didn't really erase me. If I was still in your heart and in your mind, I was never truly gone was I?"

I jump up from the bench and fan out my wings. They are black with doubt and anger. "This is a lie. This is a trick," I say confidently. I recall a voice from long ago speaking to me, "*A demon is all-knowing ... brazen, confident, manipulative, a tempter, a seducer...*"

"She was talking about Malek," Jake says matter-of-factly, "not me. I am very much real." He reaches for my hand again, and I relent. I hold tightly to him, weave my fingers in his only because I've silently dreamed of him all these years. All this time, he's been tucked away in the deepest parts of my soul, and to be in his presence makes me feel as if I'm going to burst with happiness. Here in the darkest parts of Hell, I am overcome and swelling with joy. "I am allowed to be here only because you could never get rid of me!" he chuckles his teenage boy chuckle, his familiar chuckle, his sweet and endearing chuckle.

I smile and sit back down. He takes my hands in his again, and I become dizzy and weak. "How?" I implore. "How do I know this is really you? How can you be here?"

"It's such a long and crazy story, I don't know where I would even begin. I know I had a long life. It was a good life with a lot of love and family. Tragedy, too, but the good outweighed the bad. I know I died, and it was darkness. And slowly a light flickered on in the darkness and I was made aware. I woke up somehow. I can't explain it, Aestra, but what I can say is this—I never stopped loving you. After you left Brooklyn, when I married Angela, when my daughter died, everything that happened to me, I never stopped loving you and holding you in my heart. I think that's what brought me back to you."

He takes his hand and touches the side of my face. His spirit intermingles with mine in a cool burst of energy. He is not real anymore. He is not the human of my past, but he is still the soul that speaks to my heart and memory. "You haven't changed at all," I say closing my eyes, relishing his touch. "You are different but still familiar."

He laughs. "And you've changed so much I wouldn't have recognized you!" he exclaims playfully. "But yes, you are still familiar. Regardless of your black hair, and wings, and horns, and bloodied body."

I roll my eyes at him like I had done so many times before when I was a sarcastic human—*his* human. That feeling of familiarity and humanity stings in me, and now that he is here and we are together, it is all like a dream—a dream that I have always longed to come true.

He pushes back a strand of hair from my face and looks deeply into my eyes. "Everything that has happened between us was for a reason. All of it. Every moment on Earth, in the heavens, in hell, in space and time. We were always meant to be together, Aestra." He moves in closer to me. His hot breath heavy on my neck. "We were meant to do this," he whispers, and my wholebody tenses and tingles. "This moment was meant for us. I rose up from the darkest pit of oblivion to have this moment with you."

*Could it be? Could it be possible that Lucifer brought him back? Is this the union so perfect and true that the Morning Star spoke of? The Great Teacher raised Lazarus from the dead and...*

Jake's mouth moves across my ear and down my neck in sweet, hypnotic kisses. I am entranced by his kiss, blurred by his essence and memory. I can't think straight and right now. And I don't care. I want to devour his kisses, devour his being, devour his soul.

I lie back on the stone bed ready for him, ready for his touch. He removes his clothes and comes back on top of me, kissing my mouth and throat. A cold piece of metal touches my skin and I look down to a medallion that hangs from his neck. "What's that?" I ask.

He props his upper torso up and holds it out in front of him. It's a silver charm in the shape of a diamond with the word 'Aestrangel' inscribed in the center of it. "Your necklace. The one you gave me," he says. Sure enough, it's the magic amulet, the one forged and given to me by Malek, then given to Jake by Malek, then tossed in the garbage by his jealous wife. "It's held up pretty nicely all this time, don't you think?" he jokes as he runs his hand lovingly down my chest. Dried blood flakes up from beneath his fingers, and my wings twitch underneath me. He cocks his head to the side inquisitively.

"I'm a bloody mess," I say, a wave of embarrassment flushing through me.

He shakes his head. "No way. And if you remember, the first time we were together, you were a bloody mess then too. Your face was beautifully monstrous," he sighs. "I remember the heat from your swollen face against my chest." He falls on top of me again. "Do you remember, Aestra?" he breathes. "Do you remember the first time we were together like this?"

I sigh at the thought. *How could I forget?* The memories make me shudder and swoon. The memories make me fall prey to his onslaught of kisses and his grasping hands. I collapse under his weight yet feel weightless at the same time. I am his, and I surrender to his sweetness, surrender to his tenderness.

But his gentleness reaches a maddening pinnacle and suddenly I am overwhelmed with a torrent of passion. I want to feel him all over me. I fan out my wings and wrap them around our bodies, pulling him closer to me. "You didn't have those the last time," he says with a smirk.

"I learned a few new tricks," I quip back.

I send a heated rush of yellow and orange from my feather tips and he shakes with ecstasy. My back arches, and my eyes are closed tight as I, too, am thrown into a frenzy of body-rocking spasms—so much that my wings fan back out to my sides uncontrollably.

When a metal clank hits the rock floor, Jake freezes on top of me. Suddenly, I open my eyes and see that my feathers have accidentally caught on to his medallion and flung it to the floor. His eyes go wide with terror.

"Jake?" I ask cautiously. "Jake, what's the matter?"

His image begins to fade and transform on top of me, and I am broken from my lustful trance. My eyes wake up to the truth around me as Jake Parker takes on his true demon form—a horned head of a man, stone wings unfolding from his back, and the body of a lion poised to attack. I see nothing but black as I scramble to my feet. Nothing but black as the deception becomes so obviously clear. Nothing but black as my feathers turn to spinning metal blades. Nothing but black as I hover in the air and hack away at the abomination before me. Nothing but black as the memories of his familial genocide come to the surface. Nothing but black as I bathe myself in the blood of my enemy. Nothing but black as I carve into his chest and feast upon the mass of his heart. I taste it and know that, yes, it would have been a perfect union. But I will not be deceived again. Ever.

He is now with me.

I am now with him.

His name is Jake.

And we are *becoming*.

## CHAPTER FIVE

# THE BARGAINING

This is what Jonah must have felt like being in the belly of the whale for three days and three nights. He sat there waiting and hoping for a sign from his god, atoning for his sin of betrayal and giving thanks for his life. Right now, I am Jonah sitting in the center of the Black Keep—I was commissioned a task from my master and went against his will, and now, I am left to rot in the underbelly of his domain, waiting to see if he brings me a sign of redemption or freedom. Only I am unlike Jonah because I am certainly not giving thanks to the lord our god, nor am I begging forgiveness for any perceived transgressions. I did what I had to do. And Lucifer needs to hear that loud and clear.

The three demons inside me cry out. Their lamentations echo in my head and quake in my soul. At first, I had to speak loudly in my mind's voice to silence them, but little by little, they've grown quieter until soon their voices will completely infuse with mine. Their powers have become a part of me, and soon, it will be me. It lulls like a low-frequency transmission wave in the background of my being, and eventually, I know I will double, maybe triple, in strength. For now, I am weak from trying to combine myself with newfound power and regenerating the energy I spent during my consumption of the Daimones.

Alukah stands before me in her hideous glory, and I scarcely realize she's there. The door to the Black Keep never opened, and she materialized right before my eyes. When you are Lucifer's daughter, I suppose you don't submit to the physical confines of the human world. She pulls back her black hood. Her stringy hair falls over her shoulders in matted clumps, and her hologram face flashes in slow, deliberate beats like a strobe light flickering in slow motion. It's hard not to look at her, trying to anticipate when the next facial expression will come through, but when I stare too long, she becomes a blur, and I find myself rapidly blinking my eyes to catch a new focus of her.

A *tsk* noise escapes from her jagged mouth, and she holds up her pointer finger and wags it in the air at me. "You were admonished. You were warned," she says in a sinister tone. Her voice is like two pieces of sandpaper rubbing together; it actually hurts my head to hear her speak.

"I had no control," I lie.

Her demon-clown face flashes an exaggerated frown as if to say she doesn't believe me.

"I did what I had to do."

She gingerly circles around me, strokes her claw-like fingers through my hair, and pats the tops of my wings against my shoulders. My feather tips are gray, and I wish I could hide them from her. I don't want her to see that I am in a weakened state. "You are old, but new," she muses. A piece of my hair tangles in her fingers, and with a cutting motion she clips the piece off and brings it to the center of her face where a nose should be. She inhales the scent of my hair, then scatters the locks to the ground next to me. "You are rather strange, but always true."

She rattles me. I am not afraid of her, but she makes me uneasy—uncomfortable. I stand up in defiance and meet her gaze. She is unaffected by my offensive gesture and continues to walk around, brushing up against my wings, and smelling the air around me like a bloodhound picking up a scent. Finally, she stops and something like a gasp comes from her throat. "Sixty-six inside, but really only one?" she says in a shocked voice. She pauses and moves her head lower by my chest as if she's listening for something, *speaking* to something, waiting for an answer to her question. "Two on the outside, ten on the inside?" she says to the center of my chest, but it isn't so much a question than it is a statement. After another pause, she pulls back and stands erect. Her funhouse face darkens, and I can see no trace of the Maiden, Mother, or Crone. There is nothing but a black canvas, like staring into the depths of the cosmos.

Alukah raises both her hands in front of her, and in an instant, I am lifted off the ground, suspended in mid-air. "What are you doing?" I scream in a panic as my body goes numb. She plays with me—makes me dance in mid-air. She twists and turns her hands, and my body does her will. "What are you doing to me?" I scream again, but there is music in my head now, and if she answered me, I wouldn't be able to hear her anyway.

Suddenly, my wings involuntarily crack open, and I gasp from the jolt. I have never *not* been in control of my wings, and the sensation is alien to me. The gray feathers are like clouds suspended at my sides dancing in Alukah's manufactured breeze. I try to shift my body back and forth as if I were trying to free myself from unseen bindings, but it's no use; her hold on me is strong. "Put me down, Alukah!" I yell over the music, but I can't even hear my own voice.

"Thick but hollow, both on and above ground," her voice comes through faintly, and every single feather of my wings stands up at attention as if a magnetic force is drawing them upward. There is a slight, collective tug as some of my own weight drags downward, and I am suspended only by my fragile plumes.

"Please," I beg. "Put me down and let me explain everything to the Morning Star." Even though I can't hear my voice, my desperation surprises me.

"Mighty but small. By you, the mighty fall."

The music stops, and for a second, I breathe, anticipating that Alukah will let go of her hold and send me crashing to the rocky floor. But I couldn't be more wrong. With a flick of her finger, one of my primary feathers dislodges from the delicate wing bone and floats in front of my face before flittering to the ground. A searing pain races through my wingspan, and I cry out from the heat and the pain.

"High in the sky," she says as she flicks her finger again tearing another one of my precious gray feathers from my body. "But firmly on Earth." Three. Four. Five feathers torn—the feeling so familiar, like the time I descended to Earth and took the human form. I was given false memories of a girl with a family and my wings were destroyed, obliterated.

Upon my return to Ilarium, I gained them back, but again, they were ripped from my shoulders when I renounced god. When Lucifer knighted me into his dark kingdom, they grew back—longer, stronger, darker than before. And now this: Alukah takes them from me so easily, so viciously. She strips me of my power, cuts me down from what I truly am, and leaves me defenseless against the next demon who wanders into my bedchamber.

"I will strip her naked and expose her as on the day when she was born. I will also make her like a wilderness, make her like desert land," she quotes a passage from the Bible as she tears feathers off one by one by one...

All of my nerve endings fire at once as she deliberately rips my wings apart. I dangle helplessly in the air as the gray and bright red pile beneath my feet rises. The thick blood glues the feathers together, stacking them higher and higher. Tears stream down my face uncontrollably, but *angels don't cry, angels don't cry, angels don't...*

"Stolen, then torn. Becoming something to mourn," she sings with every dainty twitch of her finger.

Arms outstretched, my head swims, rolls back from side to side. "You will pay for this," I mumble through gritted teeth, but she responds with a low laugh.

"Almost done." She plucks the last plume and with the flick of her wrist, the bones of my wings break off and crash to the floor, shattering into a million pieces like broken glass. I am released and fall into the sticky mess of broken quills, blood, and bone fragments. It meshes together and sticks against my body, covering me in a makeshift coat like a sinner who has been tarred and feathered. "An angel without her wings is strange indeed. Nubby stubs of what you used to be!"

I lunge up to strike her, but I don't have the strength. I stumble and land at her feet—a tangled, pathetic shell of greatness. "You'll regret this. Mark my words," I growl.

"You swallowed whole what you did not eat."

I narrow my eyes and steady myself on my feet again. "That's right," I say with a crazed voice. "I swallowed them all. Devoured their souls. And now I am Legion, for we are many."

She *tsks* again, mocking me. She cocks her head to the side, her kaleidoscope face now frozen on an overstated frown. "You are Aestrangel. No more. No less. One of five chosen by one of eight."

My heart sinks at her meaningless riddles, and I turn on my heel, defeated, and return to lie on the stone bed. I curl my legs to my chest and rock my swollen and bruised body back and forth for comfort. I don't pay attention to Alukah's exit.

I don't pay attention to the next daimon in my room until sometime later, either. He shambles loudly through the door, his massive weight making it hard for him to maneuver into the room. When he walks, the very ground beneath him rumbles. Covered in green scales, he shimmers like a fantastical mermaid tail, but his teeth are sharp and pointed and his breath comes out of his mouth in labored pants. He is gigantic in size—his oversized stomach hangs down to his knees, and the possibility of him killing me crosses my mind. But I don't care. Let him.

I don't acknowledge his presence—I don't look at him or speak to him, nor do I stir when he approaches and plops himself on the floor facing the bed. In one swift motion, his meaty hands stinking with rotted fish guts grab at my ankles, yank my legs apart, and drag me down on top of his lower waist. I shudder from the shock of his entrance, but indifference takes hold again, and I relax. I am still covered in bone, sand, feathers, and blood—both dried and fresh—and my mess of gore rubs gratingly and uncomfortably against his scales. But that is not important to this beast. He has one job to do.

*And I let him do it.*

Grabbing my waist, he lifts me up and down onto him, grunting and snorting with every plunge and release. His thick hands wrap around my back, and he fingers at the deep lacerations where my wings once were. Mashing his fingers in my reopened scars, he groans with pleasure as my demon blood spills into his palms. I wince at the sting of my opened wounds being violated and stay as limp as a ragdoll as he grinds between my legs. Unexpectedly, he drives one of his fingers deep into a hole in my back, rocking me with so much pain that I scream out. My reaction excites him even more as he holds me tighter, presses into me harder, and grunts louder. I pay him no mind. It seems like this assault is never-ending, and I don't have the energy to stop him or fight back. I am wingless, and without them, my power is gone.

But something catches my attention. In his supreme excitement, his fish scales illuminate the Black Keep. An energy wave pulsates off his body and encircles us in flashing green light. He's too consumed in his own pleasure to realize he's feeding me, filling me up, *healing* me. I squirm against him and adjust myself to catch his light better. My movement makes him tremble with delight, but I ignore his jerking motions. I lean forward as much as I can and rest my upper body against his protruding stomach of scales so that I can bathe my wounds in the green aura. When my body leans over as far as it can, my foot slips out from under me. Cold metal sticks to the bottom of my foot, and I contort myself to reach down and grab it. It's the medallion. Jake's medallion. My medallion. Malek's medallion.

Something ignites in me, and I put the necklace over my head, letting the diamond-shaped, inscribed face of it rest between my breasts. It rocks gently back and forth between my chest and his slimy covering. I close my eyes. His green light is drawn into the amulet like a magnet, and it fills me, lifts me. I take but a sip of it with my astral soul and snap out of my indifferent trance. Soon, the gashes on my back completely close over, and the beast can no longer slip his digits into my wounds. He gets confused, upset even. When he realizes I am no longer in pain, his light dies down, and he grunts loudly—this time not with pleasure, but with frustration. He lifts me up and slams me into him one last time before spasms overcome his body. He throws me to the corner of the room, hoists himself up, and leaves.

Again, I cry alone when the realization of what happened hits me. Yes, my power is still new, still growing, and I weep for the fact that I couldn't protect myself from Alukah's brutal attack or Fishscale's assault. But I have taken a little ounce of him with me and will keep it safe until I need it again. He is there with Mantus and Pan and Demon Jake, wrestling for space within my astral soul.

His name is Marduk.

And a piece of him is with me now.

But this is not enough. I know I will have to submit even more before I can build myself back up, but I fear I won't have the will power to do even that when all is said and done...

Three more are sent to me, and I surrender to each one. I do not fight them when they mount me. I do not struggle and squeal when they use their force. But each time I am able to catch a glimpse, inhale their demonic breath and incorporate pieces of their aura with pieces of mine. I am building my army one violation at a time. All I know is that their pieces are strengthening me, and in the process, weakening them—making for less worthy demons in Lucifer's army.

And still, there is no child to infiltrate Ilarium.

I don't think it is possible for me to reproduce. I don't think this angel-human-demon hybrid body of mine is equipped to do that. Lucifer can send the entire Order of Daimones to lie with me, and I know I would not bear.

"Why do you weep, Aestrangel?" a voice echoes in the darkness. "Is it because you are lost? Is it because you lost your wings? Is it because you failed? Is it because you defied me?" Lucifer taunts me.

The iron door swings open on its own.

"Are we done here?" I ask, my tone dripping in sarcasm. "Or have you decided to complete the job your lesser minions failed at?"

"They didn't fail, Aestrangel. You are broken somehow."

I jump up from the bed. "Broken! Have I not served you well? Have I not endured your torments for our side? I have done nothing but obeyed, and..."

"Destroyed. Ask Mantus and Pan and..."

"I no longer hear them," I lie, lowering my voice.

"You must know how much I value you, Aestrangel. I appointed you as my General, and you have served me well. I trust you and your power. You are my ideal. As the Mother of the Conqueror, you will have dominion over the heavens. I wouldn't ask this of you if I didn't think it could be accomplished. This is the only way. The Prophecy. But the Great War is coming soon, and this lack of *production* is disconcerting to say the least."

He speaks so gently; his words are soft on my ears.

"I don't think I can give you what you want," I say.

"Let's take a different approach in the matter. Let's get you out of there. Have a change of scenery. I've thought on this a while, and your demonic nature is not receptive to the creatures that spring from the Lake of Fire. We'll try one more. One more being that is closer to you in your astral gene."

## CHAPTER SIX

# THE MURDERER

**W**hen I think about it, I think the creator must have really loved me. Either that, or he had some kind of crazy point to prove. I was the only angel to have fallen from his realm twice. Twice! Not even the Morning Star can boast about that. Maybe the creator wanted to prove to everyone that I could be saved, that his most imperfect creation was *perfectly* imperfect. Or maybe he did favor me over the others? Maybe his own imperfect love had gotten the best of him, and that's why he allowed me back. Twice. Nevertheless, the creator's affinity for me and his leniency for my actions is something I'm sure Lucifer recognizes, which is why he's so intent on pulling off this mission of his. When I fell from Ilarium the first time, I was cast out into the fog-gloom world of Asphodel as punishment. Any other angel to renounce God would have been sent straight to the Lake of Fire!

Alukah has been instructed to take me back to Asphodel—the now and here, the nowhere. But this is not my Asphodel. Malek had told me that Asphodel was the place of my dreams. A holding cell, if you will—the dreamland where one could live out their days in whatever memories they could conjure. A perfect purgatory, or rather a place for Lucifer to cultivate his crew. I know. I remember all too well the pleasures and pains of my Asphodel. I had been stuck inside that Brooklyn Brownstone with the heavy sense of Jake Parker at every turn. "But he's not here," Malek had said. "Not really." And I know I wouldn't have been able to bear staying in that place, being constantly tormented by the nostalgia. The memories would have slowly driven me insane, so I decided to strike that deal with the Morning Star.

The sepia-toned sky, the acrid scent of burnt wood, and a haze of smoke filling the air let me know that, yes, this is Asphodel, but it's not mine. I'm in someone else's dream, someone else's paradise, someone else's precious memory. "Where are we?" I ask the carnival queen.

"Asking questions you know answers to," Alukah responds as she takes my hand and leads me to a sandy beach. Two moons hang low on the horizon as the tawny waves crash onto the shoreline and foam up with a thick bubbly residue left on the shells. Poison eats away at the bone of the shells, dissolving them with a vicious hiss and evaporating them into a noxious gas. A rock formation descends below the dunes, and suddenly, I'm aware of where I am. I know this place. I've been here before! This is Lilith's beach. Her place of exile when she rejected her husband Adam, the place where she fell in love with her Samael, and the place where she bore one hundred of his dead children before being able to hold a live babe in her arms.

Alukah lets go of my hand and points to the rock cave alongside the water. "Go I must. Go you shall."

I nod and walk along the toxic shore. I am wearing a long, white dress like a vision of a human woman—no longer under the protection of my strong, powerful wings, I am clothed like a common person. The venom from the surf disintegrates the bottom of the dress and burns the soles of my feet as they sink into the moist sand, but I don't care. I let the poison tickle me, let it work its way into me, let it feed a little to Mantus, and Pan, and Jake, and Marduk, and Abraxas, and Namtar, and Raum. My curiosity is piqued; I know this to be Lilith's place, and I haven't had too many dealings with the Dark Queen. Did Lucifer send me to her for inspiration of sorts?

The bones of Lilith's dead babies decorate the walls of the cave. Sand dusted from the shore has kept them shiny and smooth and secured them in place. It is a dome of fossils, specimens preserved to be studied, looked at, and remembered. A man sits at a white-bone table with legs that are fitted with tiny, deformed skulls holding it in place. When I fully enter the cave, he rises and smiles at me like he's been waiting for me.

"Aestrangel!" he sighs and approaches.

He is giant-like and towers so high that he must hunch his shoulders slightly forward so as not to hit his head on the bony ceiling. He has a head of fiery red hair that grows wildly at his shoulders and full and bushy on his face. A man, yet not. Chest muscles bulge underneath his lamb-skin tunic, and his legs are like two thick tree stumps come to life. When he moves closer toward the mouth of the cave, I notice a large scar down the side of his burly right arm like jagged lightning strikes shooting across his skin, and I know immediately from this mark who the man is.

*He is Cain. The first murderer.*

He reaches for my hand. I hesitantly grasp it, and he guides me over to the table where we sit across from each other. "I can't begin to tell you how pleased I was when the Dark Lord said we were to meet," he says with his deep voice. There's a sadness in it. A slow drawl of anger, regret, and resignation.

"I'm actually a little surprised," I reply, not knowing what else to say. He nods, acknowledging my statement, and I direct my gaze to the bone structures about the cave. They are so perfectly constructed, so perfectly arranged. Whoever built the walls must have taken a lot of time and diligence and done so with the utmost of care. It is obvious a lot of love went into this construction. "How are you here? Why are you here?" I ask. "This is Lilith's domain, isn't it?"

"This is the Land of Nod," he answers. "All wanderers and outcasts were led to this place."

"After you killed your brother, Abel," I say automatically, repeating the story so rooted in my existence.

"Yes."

I stare deeply into his dark green eyes and search for the truth. His truth. My truth. The truth that was left untold to my angelic self. The truth that was a repetitive story to my human mind. The truth that needs to be found in my demonic state.

I had always felt the story of the First Primal Murder was a curious one. In my teachings as an Angel, there were things we just *knew*. But as I grew and expanded in my own teaching and my own knowledge, the story seemed unfinished. Adam and Eve, the first man and woman began their family. Cain, their first son. Abel, their second son. Cain grew up to be a farmer, while Abel grew to be a shepherd. One day, the brothers made an offering to the creator. The lord accepted Abel's but not Cain's. Cain got jealous and took his brother out to a field where he murdered him with a rock. Then he lied to the creator about it. But instead of vengeance, the creator "marked" Cain and cast him out to wander like a nomad where he took a wife and had a bloodline and mysteriously died some time later. But that was it. Period, the end. In retrospect, the story seems vague and fragmented, like there are hidden pieces of the puzzle waiting to be revealed.

Suddenly, I think, *Cain's story doesn't have a proper ending.* Impulsively, my hand gathers my long black hair over one shoulder and rubs the thick scars where my wings once were. Defiled. Stripped. Torn. Is that how my story will end? The strange angel who fell twice from heaven. A story of trial and tribulation and an arc of greatness to be reduced to nothing but a *period, the end*? Is my true purpose to become the Mother of the Conqueror—the being who will overtake the cosmos? Is that all there is for me? To be reduced to a vessel for something else? Something better? I shudder to think...

He stares at me with a look of longing on his face. "With your hair that way and that dress you're wearing ... you look a lot like her, you know."

I ignore him and shift in my seat. "They never did say why you were denied Ishim. Why the creator refused to accept you back into his divine breath," I comment, searching his face.

"You're trying to decode the tale, aren't you?" he says with a side smile. "You think you know, but you don't know, but you do know."

I can't help but chuckle to myself. "I suppose so," I say, and I let my body relax a little. I sense he knows no other form but this human shape. There is no ugly monster to glamour away. No horns or wings to tuck and hide. No claws or scales or misshapen animal legs. When the Creator marked him, it trapped him forever in his human form. Cain is human. But not. He is daimon. But not.

*Kinda like me...*

"I'm interested to know," I say because, truly, I am.

"Walk with me," he says gently as he stands up. "Maybe all of this will become clearer." There is something about his movements, and his voice that resonates in me. Like a part of my humanness awakens around him. It's not memory, like when Demon Jake came to the Black Keep. It's more like a kinship between our dormant human spirits speaking to one another. I know he will not hurt me. Everything inside my angel mind tells me that he is the enemy, but I should pity him and pray for his salvation. Everything inside my human mind tells me that he is bad, evil, the first killer, the father of the very word "murder" and I should pray for his soul to be forever damned. Everything inside my demon mind tells me that he is lost and sad and nothing but a misunderstood historical figure...

Hand in hand, we walk out of the cave and down the poison beach. High tide is starting to come in and against the horizon, where the ocean meets the sky there are thousands of flickering jewels bobbing against the water's edge. Thousands upon thousands of dead fish pop up to the surface of the water and shimmer like the glitter of the gulf. When they reach the shore, their carcasses melt away in the deadly foam—scales melt to bone melt to fragment melt to gelatinous eyes staring into oblivion.

"Your people," I say above the sound of the pounding waves, "they were all granted Ishim, but you kind of disappeared. How come? What happened?"

We sit down on a rock ledge overlooking the ocean, breathing in the pungent sea air, yet unfazed by its toxicity. "The creator marked me," he says jerking his upper arm toward me, "after I killed Abel. I don't know why I lied about it, either, because I knew he would find out. But I was still a teenager, stupid and naïve. This was during the days when god still spoke to his people directly. When there were still so few of us in the world that we could hear his voice loudly all around us."

I reach and touch the jagged lines of his scar. Pinks and purples of raised skin are tattooed from his shoulder to his wrist like a web wrapped around his entire arm. I run my finger up and down each line of his mark, caressing the smooth, fleshy highways.

"He marked you too. This I know."

I smile sheepishly. "Continue, please."

"The mark came with a painful price," he says, retracting his arm and disengaging from my touch. "And god told me that nothing would kill me lest he would face sevenfold vengeance, but I would be forced to go to the Land of Nod to live out the rest of my days. And so here I came—to this beach, this shore, this cave. Lilith was here, had been here for many years before me, as the walls already had the remnants of her lost children. I realized she was my father's first wife—the one before my mother, the black-haired beauty with the diseased womb. She took me in but was wary of me at first. Knowing I was Adam's son, at first she thought there was some grand plot to infiltrate her home, but I assured her that I, too, had disobeyed the creator and was being punished. She came to see me as a son, and over time, I looked at her as a substitute mother. We lived together in peace in the cave—helping each other survive and living our peaceful day-to-day lives.

"I soon came to learn about Samael, her angel lover. When he came, he would send me away for forty days and forty nights while they indulged in their romance. I wandered the Earth as far east as I could go—beyond the Land of Nod, into the gloaming, to the edge of the world. And when I would come back, Samael would be gone, and Lilith would be newly pregnant. I would tend to her needs as the child grew inside of her, but she told me of the curse put on her, and I helped to mentally prepare her for the inevitable death-birth. And when the inevitable occurred, I helped her skin and filet the baby, bleach the child's bones in the sun and salt air, and arrange them in the cave as a memorial shrine. As soon as we were done, Samael returned, and I would be off again for another forty days and forty nights.

"For years this was our routine. But I was a man with the needs of a man. Every time I traversed to faraway lands, I was disappointed to see that there were no other beings like me in the world. It was sad knowing that the creator had relegated my kind to a small section of Earth where I was no longer welcome. But there was Lilith. And she was woman. One time, when I returned from one of my journeys, I expressed my frustrations to her. And from the kindness and pity of her human heart, she let me be with her.

"Samael was not pleased when he found out. Lilith was his ... and his alone. I was lucky he didn't strike me dead."

"But he couldn't!" I exclaim.

"He couldn't. He wanted to, but the Mark of the creator prevented him from harming me. I didn't blame him for feeling the way he did. If there is anything to know about the Morning Star, it is that he is fiercely protective and dedicated to what he loves. And he loves Lilith. Plain and simple."

"You and I both know he also prides himself in his retribution."

Cain scratches his thick beard. "Ah yes, this much is true. In this case, the Dark Lord went to my people and convinced my sister Awan to leave the tribe, to leave my father and mother and other brothers and sisters to come and take care of me. Awan and I left the cave to become a family of our own, but we took care of Lilith, too. I was so grateful to the Dark Lord for bringing me my Awan, I felt it was the least I could do. I owed him. I regretted laying with his love, and I was indebted to him for his kindness. So, we all stayed in Nod, and with the guidance and support from Lucifer, my sons built great cities and discovered many wonderful things. They flourished and prospered."

"But you were marked," I interject. "Marked as in unable to die. Immortal."

He sighs and tightens his grip on my hand. "Yes. I bet you can imagine the implications of that."

"You and Lilith were cast to Nod. You and Lilith are marked as immortal beings. But Awan? She came to Nod of her own volition. She would eventually..."

"Yes," he says in a low voice. "She was a loving wife. She loved our brother Abel, but she forgave me regardless. She took care of me, calmed my inner beast, worked hard, and provided me with beautiful children. For her virtue and unconditional love, she was granted Ishim when she died. As did my sons, and my grandsons, and my great-grandsons, and the line of Cain for eternity."

"But you were marked!" I repeat again in disbelief. "So why are you here in your Asphodel?"

"Because I did die, Aestrangel. The Mark lasted for seven generations. Seven-fold vengeance. For seven generations, I had to watch my family die. One by one. First Awan, then my sons Enoch, Irad, Mehujael, Methushael, and countless daughters and their children and their children. Then one day, my great-great-great grandson Lamech and his son Tubal were on a hunt. Tubal came down with a fever and went mad. Lamech carried the boy in his arms and brought him to me for a remedy. When I laid Tubal's body on the table to inspect him, I hadn't realized he was still clutching his hunting knife. The madness overcame him, and thinking I was a boar, he stabbed me, fatally, in the chest."

I pull back a bit. "And then what? What happened?"

"Lucifer came to me. He apologized for not intervening in Tubal's actions. He told me there was a place for me in his kingdom if I wanted it. I told him that I had to wait and see what the creator wanted from me, and then I would make my eternal decision."

"And the lord said..."

"Nothing. Absolutely nothing. I waited to hear his voice for a very long time. I drifted in and out of Asphodel looking for any kind of clue or sign. I implored him to give me some kind of guidance. But there was nothing. Just silence. And so, I made my choice. Lucifer granted me dominion over the Terrene Apokomistai—the land dwelling demons—and I have served him well since."

"For what? To what end?" I question.

Cain leans back and exhales deeply. "The tale needs to be finished, doesn't it?"

I pause, the lens slowly coming into focus. Is Cain's story set to have a proper ending with mine—with his role being the Father of the Conqueror? Two humans turned demon with a hint of angelic blood. Oh, the little monster we could create! Is that where this is going? Is that what Lucifer meant by *"One more being that is closer to you in your astral gene?"*

I look away from him and stare at the glittering death floating on top of the water. My stomach drops and I, too, am bobbing helplessly on the ocean's waves. "Are you saying the end of your story will be the same as mine?" I say in a faraway voice. But I know the answer to that. The truth has been revealed. "What did the Morning Star tell you will come of this?" I ask, still looking to the horizon. But I know the answer to that as well.

For a lifetime, Cain has suffered the loss of his family. In a jealous rage, he killed his own brother, was separated from his parents and siblings, reunited with his sister, and had a happy life with her only to watch her and their children die, until finally he was abandoned by the creator. I'm sure the prospect of fathering the Great Conqueror sounds like a dream come true for him. Cain would finally be a part of a family that would not only make an impact on the world but also would be remembered for ages to come. Not just an unfinished story. Not just a fizzled-out legend. Not just a disintegrated school of fish fragments washed up on a distant shore.

He stands up and holds out his hand. "Come back with me to the cave, Aestrangel. We can figure all that out there."



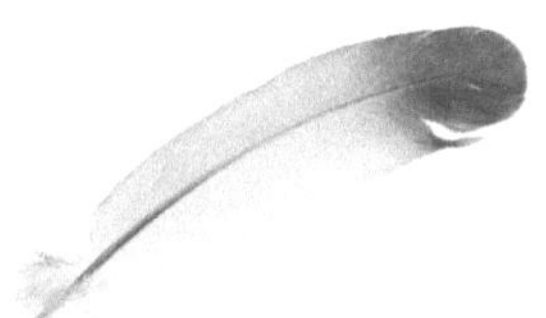

## CHAPTER SEVEN

# THE LOVER

If this is my story—if this is the beginning of a crescendo and an end—I want to do things my way. Mine alone.

Our stroll along the beach is a lingering one; we stop every now and then to take in the seaside scenery, marvel at the unnatural splendor of Asphodel, and talk a little bit about our lives in our many different roles. He's courting me like any good-natured man would. He stares at me longingly with his deep green eyes. They twinkle and sparkle like the death-laden ocean, and for all his humanness, I am still acutely aware that he is demon—ruler of scores of the damned just as I have been appointed to lead Lucifer's army in the Great War. We are one and the same, Cain and I, and he is proving to be a potential suitor.

My preternatural senses are not quite completely smitten with his charms, but in all honesty, the way he smoothly speaks to me, the way he caresses my shoulders and runs his fingers down the side of my neck are all too familiar. It's all too human.

"I remember a time when all I could think about was being one of them—a human—when my only goal was to have a real, human dream and descend from The Observatory and be the champion for the Creator's most intense design. I remember how I had longed to be part of the human world and to spread my divinity among their ranks. I was so enamored with them that I couldn't see beyond their ugly inherent nature. I excused their cruelties. I looked past their flaws. I convinced myself that the creator knew what he was doing in his supreme design and that everything happened for a reason and that there was perfection in their imperfections.

"And then I was slammed with the truth.

"Humans are nothing but the creator's experiment—a dash of this, a sprinkle of that. And I was infected so deeply with it that I can't seem to shake it now. It has become a part of me—a part of my entire existence."

"Don't lose that part of you," Cain says clasping my hands in his and bringing them up to the space between our chests. I realize I've been blabbering to him this whole time, opening up to him about parts of me I've never let anyone else know about.

"Why?" I ask. "Humanity is a stain. A curse. It kept me weak when I should have been able to protect myself. It made me second guess some of my actions."

"But it makes sense for us, doesn't it?"

I pause and think on it. "I suppose."

"How many demons did the Morning Star send to you? How many demons tried to make you their mate? How many demons tried to subdue you and father the Conqueror?"

I think of them all, tucked away inside of me. I think of the demons I consumed and obliterated and those whom I stole a piece of their essence. It makes me smile.

"Did you think why they were all unsuccessful?" he continues. "In order for the Conqueror to be successful in his mission, he will need a spark of humanity. The creator has such a soft spot in his heart for them, and it will be hard for him to destroy your son, a child no less."

I huff out a gust of air in the most human way possible. "Are you saying I'm not human enough?" I bark.

"Like that's a bad thing?" He laughs and draws me closer to him. He puts his hand on the back of my neck and guides my face to his chest, his beard resting at the top of my head. He is much larger than I am—it's as if I am being swallowed in his embrace. His tunic is opened at the front, and my ear rests against his taut muscular shell. I listen to the ocean waves crash on his inside. The rise and fall of his every breath is like the ebb and flow of the tide. "The part of you that is still human is screaming to the part of me that is," he sighs, and his voice echoes from some chamber deep within him like noise reverberating off cavern walls. "We need this, you and I. We need this to be the shining moment to our legacies. Lucifer wills it so. So mote it be."

I tilt my head upward and look dreamily into his eyes. *This is so wrong. Everything about this is so wrong.*

He returns my dreamy gaze with one that is gentle and sweet. He sweeps his massive hand across my cheek and lets his fingers dance softly on the side of my face. There is no malice in his touch, no rush to copulate like wild animals, just two beings enjoying each other's auras and conversation and company.

"Were you truly sorry for what you did to your brother?" I ask.

Cain pulls back a little and my fingers dig into the skin on his back from his movement. "Of course, I was; that's why I was marked. It was the least He could do. Abel was a vain boy who gloated often. He was *wrong*. And while my actions were wrong in the eyes of the Creator, my guilt was too much to bear, so he spared me. Punished me. But spared me."

I nod my head. I was spared too. Punished. But spared. I know all too well. I slip my hand under his lambskin tunic and run my fingertips up the length of his back, feeling it blossom with goosebumps.

"You cling to your humanity like a safety blanket," he continues. "Humanity was all I knew until the creator showed me his true face. Once I saw the truth, that he wasn't the all loving, all-merciful father my parents had portrayed him to be, it lit up something inside me. Something so vile and wretched it couldn't be controlled."

"And thus, you turned to the Morning Star for your salvation."

Suddenly, he swoops me up into his arms like a husband would do to his new wife. "Enough of this talk, though," he says. "We have other matters to attend to." And with that, I see past the fog gloom of Asphodel and beyond the burnt sky. Cain was the only demon who has shown me kindness and friendliness and genuine care and...

*Humanity.*

He still reeks of it. The scent is very heavy in his aura, and I surmise that even with the mark of the creator and even with his demonic transformation, Lucifer couldn't erase the core of what Cain was, regardless of his wickedness. The man in him lusts for me, and in his mind, he's courted me enough. *But I was a man with the needs of a man,* he had said.

And then, something Cain said earlier strikes me deep, *"How many demons tried to subdue you?"* And I feel shame—shame for allowing this to go as far as it has, shame for agreeing to Lucifer's diabolical plan, shame for not holding my ground and consuming the souls of every single godforsaken creature who dared to even look at me sideways!

He is more human than I. I am Aestrangel, and he is beneath me.

When we return to the cave, he carries me over the threshold in some notion of human romanticism—as if this simple act is going to make me succumb to his advances. Make me submit to his desires. But I have flipped the script. We are no longer in the bone-riddled cave of Lilith's lost children. We are no longer in Cain's Asphodel.

*We are in mine.*

He gently releases me onto the floor as his mouth goes agape with confusion and wonder. "W... Where are we?" He stutters in disbelief.

I've re-created the brownstone—my bedroom in Aunt Ruth's dwelling. The place I stayed when I was a human. The bed I first sinned upon. "My home," I say. "I thought you might like to see where human girls thousands of years after your time liked to stay."

He laughs. "Oh Aestrangel, I've seen much. I know of the modern world. I don't understand how we..."

"I will it so. So mote it be," I reply, echoing his previous words.

Cain's eyes go wide, the sea green color flashing wildly in the dim-lit room. There is so much power in them. I feel it. He tightens his lips together, a loss for words, and his red beard juts out from his chin. There is a desire in his giant eyes, a desire written all over his humanly demon face, and I know he wants a taste of my soul.

I move to the bed and tug my cotton dress at the shoulders. It falls to the floor, and I stand there naked. My hands shake in anticipation as I extend my arms out at my sides so that he can get a better look at me. Energy boils up from the pit of my stomach, and I radiate a glorious golden glow around me, waiting to gobble him up, waiting to engulf him in my light and bring him pleasure unimaginable.

He doesn't move a muscle. He's frozen in awe, fixated on my angelic glory. "I... I don't know what to say," he stammers like a frightened schoolboy, and a part of me is disgusted by his human innocence.

"You've been around a while. I'm sure you can figure it out," I say coyly.

Without further hesitation, he removes his tunic and pants, readying himself to be fully encompassed in my light. He is entranced, spellbound with my beauty, so enthralled with my power that he doesn't even notice a shift in the room. It's a slight movement in the fog, like a temperature change or like someone slightly shaking a snow globe. But I noticed it. I sense we are being watched by some outside force. Possibly we are being monitored to make sure that this pairing doesn't go the ways of the others who attempted to breed with me.

"It's okay to bring out your demon side, ya know," I say playfully, and I see him catch his breath. He takes a cautious step forward, a few inches outside of my golden light. He hesitates like a child standing on the edge of the ocean for the first time. *<I don't bite,>* I say, but not out loud. I say it directly to his mind, and he smiles when he receives my message.

*But I do.*

*And I will.*

Again, he gingerly moves closer, but he is struggling to contain his excitement. He is a gigantic specimen in every imaginable way, only I have no intention of having any carnal knowledge of the demon man, Cain.

He reaches his hand out, his fingertips dip into my light, and he shudders with pleasure, but before he gets a chance to fully enjoy the brief moments of energy I had planned on sharing with him, someone comes up from behind, knocking him onto the bed. Immediately, I stop my flow of gold, and step to the side.

It's Malek. He stands before me; his eyes sweep over my naked body, and he smirks with perverted approval. I roll my eyes, cover my exposed breasts with my hands, and stamp my foot on the floor. "What the hell are you doing?"

"Shut up!" he barks. "There's not much time. He'll be up soon."

"You know who this is, right?" I yell in disbelief.

Malek moves to Cain's unconscious body face down on the bed. "Yes. And you know who I am, right? You know who *you* are, right?" He outstretches Cain's arms and begins tying them together with barbed wire. The flesh of Cain's wrists shred up like grated cheese, and his blood falls messily to the hardwood floor. Aunt Ruth would be so mad at this mess...

"How did you get here?" My questions seem so trivial considering the scene unfolding before me.

"I always know where to find you. You know that!"

*Yes. Yes, I do.*

"So now what? What happens next? When Lucifer finds out..."

"This is Asphodel, Aestrangel. We're guarded here. It's fine. You're going to do what you did to the others."

I roll my eyes again. "I was going to do that anyway!"

Malek stops fussing with Cain's arms and pulls back a little. His face twists up. "You were?"

"Yes!" I yell again.

"B... But it seemed like..." he stammers.

"Are you for real? Are you kidding me right now? I was going to take care of it! You know I can handle myself!"

"It's just that... I don't know... your light... the way you were talking, and..."

My aura flashes gold again. The strong energy shoots out all around me in every direction "Were you *spying* on me, Malek Forcas?"

Around him, a light gray aura pulsates, and in flashes, I catch glimpses of his human self and his true form. I know he's struggling to hide the beast from me, but he is at a moment of pure vulnerability, and he's at war within himself. "I don't know," he repeats. "I couldn't get to you in the Black Keep, and I couldn't..."

*Because. He loves you too much.* The Dark Lord's words race back into my head. And it is clear. Malek came to help me ... because he loves me. He's always loved me. He always will love me. Everything he said to me was a lie, a front, a way to push me away and not confront the reality of what was about to happen to me. Demons *can* love. Even the evilest and most pure of them.

"Thank you," I say, lowering my hands from my chest. We stare at each other for what seems like a long while until he finally rushes over to me and pulls me into a strong embrace. His claws desperately scratch up and down my back as if he never wants to lose the feeling of them again, and he squeezes his arms around mine so tightly that I feel as if I can't breathe. His gray pulsates with my gold into a beautiful, swirling metallic color that raises us off the faux floor. My scars tickle. My shoulder blades twitch. And the warmth of Malek's love breathes happiness to the depths of my soul.

"Go to him," he says, looking at Cain on the bed.

"Only with you."

Malek and I sit opposite from each other with Cain's body between us. The metal aura swirls like a maelstrom around us, encompassing us. Malek turns Cain's body face up, and I place my hands right above Cain's stomach—the pit of his humanity. Malek then places both of his hands on my shoulders.

*And we sing.*

Great dirges and hymns of lamentations. We open ourselves to the swirling darkness, our souls caressing one another in a passionate, ethereal kiss. Swaying to the sounds of the dying souls in the Lake of Fire and the moaning torments from the Hall of Punishment. They are all one within me. Within us. Malek is with me now. A piece of him flows into me in a maelstrom of chaos. A piece of me filters into him as well. And all of Cain sucks back up to the void of nothingness and dissipates with the others who have dared to step foot on my terrain. The lullaby soothes me, filling me with forbidden love and shadowy hope. I dance with Malek in our otherworldly state, imbued with an evil I never had imagined.

We sing until the very last pieces of Cain are incorporated in me, until his eyes go black with the undeniable gloom of death. And then *he* sings to me. On the inside. Along with Mantus, Pan, and Jake, and Marduk, and Abraxas, and Namtar, and Raum.

He is now me.

I am now him.

His name is Cain.

Cain. The first murderer.

And we are *becoming.*

But I feel something else stir inside of me. Something deep in my abdomen. It swirls around like a candle flame and startles me so much that I cease the energy transmission with Malek. There's a new energy that invades my essence.

"What's wrong?" Malek asks when I pull away from him.

"I don't know. I felt something. Inside."

"You're growing, Aestrangel. Nothing to worry about."

"Do you think one of them could have..."

Malek shakes his head wildly back and forth.

I sit up at attention, frantic. "There's no way there's a child..."

He shakes his head more fervently. "Absolutely not. It's a new energy source. A silver energy. Strong. Metal. Weaving..."

"Us?"

"Maybe."

He leans over Cain's lifeless body and kisses me hard on the mouth. His jagged fangs scrape my bottom lip, and he laps at the tiny blood bubbles with his forked tongue. Just like his father's.

# -PART II-
# THE CHOSEN

*"Well, there is one thing I am certain of—there will be no more Callings for you. You will be assigned another role which has not yet been determined, but it must be something special as the Lord has chosen you from the beginning of time. Now that you are back, we can all begin anew—a fresh start. We can make things right again."*

—CAMAEL

CHAPTER EIGHT

# THE GENERAL

The sun crests over the horizon, and the first rays of the dawn filter their way into the window of my bedroom. Malek lies next to me in a peaceful dream state. My arm drapes over his heavy chest and bobs up and down with his every breath. Deep inhales and smoky exhales. I scarcely wonder what he dreams about, or if he even dreams at all. I'm guessing the latter because I can't remember the last time I had a conscious dream. I think sleep for our kind is more of a re-charge than anything else. We technically don't have to sleep, but we do anyway. Regardless, I'm awake now, concentrating on every second the sun creeps up higher and the room is filled with more and more light. I rather enjoy this quiet solitude, and do not wish for him to stir awake yet. Sometimes, I prefer to be alone with my own thoughts. It's something I'm quite accustomed to.

Cain's remains are stuffed under the floorboards beneath our bed in some strange allusion to the human poet someone long ago called the Birdman. I'm not sure what we needed to hide, or why we even bothered to bury him, but both of us agreed that it was the best thing to do. *The best thing to do?* If there ever is such a thing... especially when you're demons such as we are. Perhaps there was a malicious side to having his body underneath us as we indulged in the pleasures of our flesh night after night. Perhaps there was an added rush of power or even a hint of disobedience in our actions.

Whatever the case may be, Malek and I also decided to remain in Asphodel—to hide away from everyone and everything in my personal fog-gloom heaven. Here, we've taken full advantage of our privacy and used this time however we've pleased. We've satiated one desire after the other. If our minds have dreamed it, we've done it. We quickly learned that my Asphodel was no longer limited to the brownstone construction—that with Malek here and by combining our powers, we were able to travel to faraway lands in the distant past and future. We visited other worldly beings in deep space dimensions, alternate realities and timelines. Combined, our energy force is magnanimous as we were able to take our new knowledge, learning to create and shape Asphodel as we saw fit. No longer can I manifest power orbs in the palm of my hands, but now I have the power to create, shapeshift, change. Malek and I have spent hours as phoenixes chasing each other's fire trails against a black ink sky. We have created oceans of pink waves that crash upon shores of blue sand as seven-legged star creatures scuttle in between our cloven hooves. It's magnificent the wonder we've fashioned! We've become our very own creators of our very own world ignoring our duties and obligations to whatever higher power has their clutches on our souls. We are our own gods. But I fear our time together will be coming to a close.

*And it's been forty days and forty nights.*

Malek stirs under my arm, and I know he will be awake soon. It is his usual pattern of movements right before he opens his eyes. I shift my leg over his waist, and he's so massive my toes can barely touch the bed beside him. But I want to hold on to him. Hold on to this moment as tightly as I can and squeeze the energy source right out of him and into me before anyone takes him away from me.

In the pit of my stomach, the new energy continues to grow and get stronger with every passing day. During one of our lengthy conversations, Malek and I surmised that it's a by-product of those I've taken—a tangled mass of different powers converging within. And with every passing day, I can hear songs and conversations and whispers and an electric hum blossoming in me. It grows. Strong. Stronger. Strongest. I've trained myself to control it lest it would completely consume me and drown me in its silver light. And while it may not be the child that Lucifer had wanted me to bear, I feel it is the power of something more worthy, more dynamic, more powerful than I could have ever imagined. I have affectionately named the energy Apophis—for it is a god of chaos that swirls and slithers in my belly like an evolving snake. Malek has even said that he fears the day when I decide to unleash this power on the world! I can only imagine...

Before I realize what's happening, Malek's eyes widen, and he shoots up from the bed. His brow furrows down at me in a disapproving way, and I terminate my energy flow. I must have drifted into a temporary trance because when he moves away from my grip, the remnants of my metallic aura flicker and fade. "I... I'm sorry," I say apologetically. "I didn't..."

He grins at me. "Trying to suck me dry like the others, Aestrangel?"

"No, no, no!" I say frantically.

He pets my head to calm me down. "It's okay. I understand," he says with a chuckle.

Because he does. He understands that my power has far surpassed his own. He understands that I want to stay with him right here for the rest of eternity (because he wants the same thing too). And he understands that our rendezvous in Asphodel is coming to a close.

"Did I hurt you?" I ask.

"Hurt me?" he bellows with a hearty laugh. "You can never hurt me, Morning Glory."

I smile and slither my body closer to him. I wrap myself into the crook of his arm and nuzzle my face hard against his chest. He exhales loudly, and the shape of his body shrinks down to his human form—the jet-black hair and stormy gray eyes that captivated (and repulsed) me all those years ago. My bottom lip puckers out in protest of the change. "What? No good?" he questions. "I thought you loved me as a man in his manly body," he laughs with human sarcasm.

I can't help but giggle at his tone. "Oh, I do," I say, sitting up. "I've just gotten so used to *you*. The real you."

"Ahh, so you love the beast more?" he sighs.

I stare longingly at his human form and run my fingers down his bare chest stopping at every crease and crevice of his hard definition. I take him in, a vision of demonic beauty and perfection. I want to inhale him, drink of him, save him for myself, keep him for me and only me. I do everything in my power to keep from pulling at his aura like a magnet. "No," I respond in a faraway voice, "all of it."

He grins and nods his head. We both know it's time. "He called to me last night," he says after a moment of silence. I know he's referring to the Morning Star.

"So? He's called to us every night," I say matter-of-factly.

"I know, I know, but this time was different. This time was…"

"Stop. Don't say it," I plead.

"The War is coming, Aestrangel. That's inevitable. The signs are all there, and we've been absent for far too long, and…"

"You want to go?" I say in disbelief, cutting him off.

"What do you think? But we're no longer at the mercy of what we want. We can't ignore our roles in what's to come. Ideally, I would forsake everything and everyone to spend the rest of eternity here with you. But you and I both know that that's not possible."

I hang my head, still unwilling to face the truth. "I know," I say in a low voice. Because I do know. Lucifer has been in my head since Malek and I never returned to Gehenna, and for the most part, I've been able to tune him out. But not so much anymore. I know what Malek means. There's much at stake, and both he and I have an integral part to play in the impending battle.

He rolls over and off the bed. "Where shall we spend our last morning in Asphodel? Beach? Mountains? Bright Angel Trail?"

I turn to the edge of my side and bend forward with laughter. "Bright Angel Trail?" I exclaim. "You're really wanting to go down memory lane, aren't you?"

But there's no response from him. His silence sends a chill into my heart, and the snake squirms in my belly. I snap my head around and see he is frozen in his tracks, staring at me. "What? What's the matter?"

He points to my back. "You... you can't feel them?"

"What? Feel what?" I say as my arm reaches up behind me. I, too, freeze when my hand touches the slight extensions of cold steel at my back. "Is it...?"

"Your wings," he says, and I can hear the smile in his voice.

*My wings.*

My glorious, powerful wings. Given to me by the creator. Torn from me on my descent to Earth. Granted back to me on my return to Ilarium only to be ripped off during my rejection of the lord. Then reconstructed into a thing of black beauty by Lucifer only to most recently be shredded by Alukah to neuter me. I've had such a long and painful relationship with these things of mine. And now, after all the trauma, they are coming back to me— of my own design. Not the design of the creator. Not the design of the Morning Star. Mine. My will. My power. I guess I didn't feel it because I've been so numb to that part of me, but sure enough, here they are. Cold. Steel. Metallic like the aura that circles me. I envision what they will be when they have fully grown—robust alloy appendages transforming at my resolve. Strong and sturdy. I know no one will ever be able to strip them of me again.

Malek and I never do have our last stroll in Asphodel. We leave right from the brownstone and go back to the throne room in Gehenna to confront the Dark Lord. Lucifer sits patiently in his chair as if he knew we would be arriving at that moment. He breathes a sweet-smelling smoky aura of grays and blacks that dances around the foot of the throne. Alukah stands between his chair and mine, one hand on the back of her father's headrest and the other impatiently tapping my empty space, with her hood covering her face. Lilith circles her throne bed in the corner of the room. Her massive tail sways and gently rattles defensively when we approach Lucifer.

He claps his hands. "Ahhh, the Dark Lovers have returned."

Something like a blush of flowers on my cheeks, and I remember Camael's teachings from long ago: *"See everyone, that is raw and tangible emotion, one that humans feel regularly. Shame, guilt, embarrassment, all can come on in that way."* I lower my head instinctively to hide my face from him.

"Father..." Malek begins, but Lucifer holds up his hand to silence him.

"I am not angry, if that's what you're going to ask. You don't need to explain, either. Who am I to put limits on my children? The very essence of this entire existence is based on self-indulgence, hedonism, excess..." his voice trails off in a hissing sound that echoes in the cave, and he brings his long, white fingers together pensively. "I should have known keeping you two apart wasn't the best of plans, but I assure you, I had only the best of intentions. No harm done though, children," he exhales, and the scent of sweet, rotted flowers permeates the air around him. "Lord knows I have a weakness of my own." He turns and glances lovingly at Lilith. "But now we have other matters that need to be addressed."

I stand up straight at attention, hoping the folds of my flesh and my long black hair will somehow mask the metal nubs sprouting from my scars. "I'm sorry for what I've done," I say firmly because I know he will be expecting some form of apology.

"Sorry?" he asks, screwing his perfectly chiseled face to one side. "Sorry for decimating some of my finest warriors? Sorry for rendering great soldiers useless in the upcoming war? Sorry for reducing one of my favorite servants to nothing but an empty shell stashed under a wedding bed? Sorry for wielding your fantastic and great power? Sorry for being *you*, Aestrangel?"

I shudder to think of what will come next from his lips, and I brace myself for an onslaught of wrath. Malek, too, tenses a bit next to me. "You need not be sorry, dear. You need to kill that part of you that is so married to your former angelic life. While they are nice and appreciated, I do not require apologies."

My shoulders relax, and Malek sighs lightly.

"But you were right, I failed you," I continue, brazen and unafraid. "There is no child. No pure demon entity to infiltrate Ilarium."

"Ah, yes. This much I know. You could not attain the one goal I had set for you."

"An oak whose leaf fades away. Or a garden that has no water," Alukah interjects, reciting human Scripture again. "A barren womb, not ever to create. The only thing left is death, our fate."

"Hush, child!" Lucifer says to her from the corner of his mouth. "There are some things worse than death," he outstretches his arms to me, "and one of them is you," he says with a slick grin.

I go to him, clasp his hands, and he spins me around in front of him, inspecting me, taking me in, basking in my power and glory. "We will still mobilize in preparation for the War."

Lilith shoots me a wicked look. "But she cannot conceive! She cannot create!" she cries from her corner.

"Oh, but she can!" Lucifer coos. "She can create famine, and disease, and destruction, and war." He spins me around one more time for his enjoyment. "Her power has tripled in strength, and she could punch a hole right through the world if she wanted to. Couldn't you, Aestrangel?" he says with a sly tone.

I nod.

I can.

He releases my hands, and I sit next to him in my chair, my rightful place as his second in command. "The Nekudaimones sing to me," he continues. "The Empyreal Order of the Atmosphere tell me the Powers That Be speak of a parlay. Rumors swirl that they wish to meet on common ground to bargain a truce of sorts. Do I believe in this virtuous agreement? Absolutely not. Aestrangel, as my Supreme General, I am ordering you to ready the other Commanders. As leader on the battlefield the others will take their orders from you. Devise a strategy and prepare your forces. Other than me, you are the only one who has knowledge of their ranks and inner workings. Use that in your favor. Use that against them.

"Malek, my boy, The Knight of Hell, the Prince of Gehenna, he who commands twenty legions of the finest fighters of Hades—your team is now under the command of Aestrangel. I am sending you above, commissioning you to strike an agreement with the Watchers. Because of your many interactions with them and your proclivity for the human experience, they will be most receptive to you. Broker a deal. Create a plan. Do everything in your demonic power to make them see things your way, but do not promise anything. The only agreement you should abide to is time and place. They will want peace, but I have a feeling they will want to barter—make an exchange of sorts for the murder of Camael. We will have to do what we will have to do, and if the opportunity arises, we will strike. Under Aestrangel's guidance, we will take action if we have to.

"And even if we don't."

# THE ARMORER

Lucifer waves his hands and dismisses us from his court. I rise, bow to him, step down from the stage, and walk over to Malek to bid him goodbye. Alukah and Lucifer both make their way down the tunnel of the throne room, and Lilith lies lazily on her bed.

One thing I do find very interesting and odd is that Lucifer hadn't recognized the change in me. He noted that my power has tripled in size, yet he never specifically mentioned the *physical* change—the growing power that coils in my abdomen like an actual child developing and twisting and strengthening inside. *Apophis*. The menagerie of spirits conjoined within—a new entity who is constricting and consuming what's left of the lesser deities.

Still, my stomach flopped when Lucifer said he was sending Malek away, and an icy shock jolts my body again at the thought. We've been inseparable for so long. I'm not sure if I can handle him leaving, especially under these conditions, with the threat of war imminent. A part of me is afraid to be alone, and a part of me is afraid to lose him.

"You're kidding me, right?" he says with a furrowed brow. My consternation must be written all over my face.

"What?" I say in the high-pitched voice of a naïve human teenager. It's not really a question though, because I know *he* knows that *I* know what he's talking about.

He places his hands on my shoulders and looks me deep in the eyes. They are black as night and I can see my own reflection within, but it's not really my reflection of the now and here—it is the altered image of the nowhere, and in this altered image, I am smiling and laughing and dancing in a sunflower field. My dark cotton dress flows along the grassy land, and my black hair sweeps in between the bright yellow petals of the flowers. I spin around and around and around, and as I am dancing, a little black-haired boy peeks from behind my dress. He giggles and hides and giggles and reappears in a simple game of peek-a-boo. Is this my child? Malek's child? A physical representation of Apophis? The what-could-have-been? The little boy's eyes are jet black like Malek's, and I glance into them, going further into the image. There I see my reflection of the now—long black hair flung over my back, the craggy cave walls behind me, and a look of worry and doubt on my face. Malek has whittled himself into my mind and is showing me a mirage of my own desires. Not nice to play with my emotions like that! I shake my head to rid myself of the images and he smiles. "Separation anxiety?" he says. "Don't tell me you're losing your edge."

"I guess you're right," I say, somewhat defeated. "I'll miss you. For what it's worth."

He leans in and kisses me on the forehead. "For what it's worth," he says and walks past me down toward the tunnel.

I turn on my heel and head in the same direction. Malek is right. I need to regain the confidence inside myself that I once had. I think I am losing my edge a bit, and I have to do something to get it back in order to do what needs to be done. Now and ultimately.

Before I reach the archway of the tunnel, Lilith glides down from her throne bed and in front of my path. Her snake tail rattles gently as she slowly moves toward me. She glistens in the dim light of the cave—the greens and yellows of her snakeskin sparkle with an iridescent hue. From the waist up, she is beautiful to look at, a young woman preserved. She is flawless and frozen in time. From the waist down, she is a stunning sight to behold— the slow-moving body of Medusa slithering at a leisurely pace, revealing her status as an ancient being. For eons, she has embodied this form—the first human woman borne from the creator's earthly soil turned into one of the first demonic beings to rule Hell. She and I have more in common than I had originally thought.

"Too close," she hisses at me in a low voice.

I cock my head to the side inquisitively, and she begins to circle me. A trail of ooze follows her on the stone floor, binding me to the area, forbidding me to leave. I take a step back, and when the heel of my foot touches the substance it sends an electrical shock up my leg.

"Too close, you and the boy," she repeats as she glares at me with a look of contempt.

She's referring to Malek, and I think, *What a complete act of motherhood for her to refer to her thousands year old son as "the boy."*

"I don't understand," I say.

"Yes, you do. You know exactly what I mean." She slithers her upper body into the circle she's created and moves her head and torso back and forth in front of me. The Snake Queen smells earthy, like a sweet pungent scent of jasmines and dirt. Is she still connected to the human world? When I plagued the soil spreading famine and disease, did she feel that too? Did I poison a part of her as well?

And she hates me. I know this much. I sense this much. I knew it from the first moment I stepped foot in the throne room. She had glared at me hard with a look of maddened rage and a side of jealousy. My body tenses when she slinks closer to my abdomen and freezes. Her head moves in circles about my waist, and her nostrils flare wide as she inhales my aura. I close my eyes tightly, trying to block her out from intruding into my mind or rooting around in my astral gene. Suddenly, she pulls back, pauses with a look of confusion on her face, and she continues her circular dance around me. "Harden your heart, or you will forget your true self," she continues.

"I know my true self very well, thank you," I say.

She nods in agreement. "But it's easy to forget... especially when you are invested in someone else." She pauses and sniffs the air around me. "When you are invested in some*thing* else."

She senses something, I know, but she can't quite put her snake tail on exactly what it is. Lilith had said I couldn't conceive, and for the most part, she was correct. I can't conceive—not in the traditional sense. Not in the way she has for millennia after millennia. But I can create. I have created life—a life force that brews inside me like a weapon waiting to be unleashed. She can't figure it out because the creation of Apophis is unprecedented. And she doesn't recognize it as a threat because it is a part of her, too. Apophis has a part of Malek's astral gene, thus in turn being a part of both Lucifer and Lilith. Maybe that's why the Morning Star was blind to the newest addition?

The ooze on the floor starts to dry away, and I watch it disintegrate so that I can make my move and leave her presence. "I will stay the course, no need to worry about that," I say.

"Samael is counting on you," she says. "He chose you. Many, many, years ago when you were but a speck of stardust in the cosmos. Samael always knew it would be you. He saw a darkness in you before you were even formed—a darkness that filled his heart and excited him, for it rivaled his own. He chose you above all."

I take my opportunity to step free of her magic cage. "The same way he chose you?" I ask, bitingly.

She arches her head back, and the skin of her perfectly white throat pulls taut against her larynx. Blue and green veins run jagged up and down her neck and chest as she lets out a haunting chuckle. "He didn't choose me, Aestrangel. I chose him."

I turn away from her and make my way to the arch of the tunnel. "Go to the Armorer," she calls to my back, and I hear the crunch and crackle of baby bones on her bed— the sounds of the Dark Queen resting herself back on her throne, but I don't look back at her. "He has something for you that you will need."

—✕—✕—✳—✕—✕—

The Armorer's grotto is right beyond the Hall of Punishment. Fires burn in every smoke-filled corner, and

minion demons toil tirelessly in service to Vulstus, the leader of this domain. He notices me right away when I peek my head in from one of the alcoves, snaps his fingers so his underlings stand at attention, and waves his hand for me to enter the forge. Vulstus does not speak, for legend has it he sacrificed his tongue and pledged a code of silence to Lucifer. He is an Apokomistai Daimon of the order Lucifugi, the nocturnal—an old one, one of the first and highest-ranking demons.

He grunts at me as his own armor clanks with his every movement. On closer inspection, though, he's not wearing any armor. His very skin is made of metal and chains! The helmet on his head is his actual skull with his eyes and nose exposed against the opening of the metal plated viewfinder. "I was told you have something for me," I say, and he nods with a clashing din.

He waves his arms in the air, and his workers scuttle around the forge pulling from the shelves, opening drawers, disappearing into cubby holes and emerging with pieces of copper and iron. They are quick and nimble on their hind legs and make good use of their prehensile tails. Their little bodies remind me of the human vision of elves—little workers who serve the man in the red coat, only these little devils serve the man in the red steel.

Vulstus holds my arms out at the sides and in a flash the little ones are all over me with their miniature tools. They hammer away tinkering at fasteners, putting interlocking pieces of metal together, screwing layer upon layer into place. I almost lose my breath at how quickly they work. When they are done and jump down from my newly outfitted body, I look down at my new garb. A strong steel breastplate the color of blood comes up to my chin with pointed spikes. The half-skulls of fallen warriors encased in gold are nestled at each shoulder, and the golden-plated armor goes as far down as my knees.

But it is too tight against my chest, and I wiggle a bit. Vulstus sees me struggling and holds my arms out again, trying to figure out what's wrong. My wings have grown a little more, and the bodice is uncomfortable against my steely branches. "It's too tight," I say, and he waves his hands again. The devils surround me, unfastening and pulling apart their work. Some grumble and huff, some speak in a high-pitched, ancient tongue. When I am dis-robed, I turn around and pull my hair forward, exposing my own growing armory. "You see now?" I ask, and Vulstus gasps in surprise. He takes the breastplate from one of his minions and goes to one of the workstations. Sparks and flames encircle him as he burns holes through the plates. Then he himself brings the armor back over and places it over my head, knighting me proper as a Commanding General. This time, when the metal touches my skin and rests gently on the edges of my wing stubs, I feel whole. I feel strong.

It is a perfect fit.

The minions bring me a copper shield emblazoned with the seal of Lucifer—the upside-down broken star with a 'v' shape underneath—to signal to my enemies whom I serve. Some other workers hand me a thick sword with an intricately carved hilt—one that depicts the souls of the damned clawing their way out of Gehenna. "I don't need these," I say, confused.

Vulstus nods as if to say "Yes, you do."

"No really, I..." I begin to protest, but he places his hands on the skulls at my shoulders, and a great tumult of wind rushes in my ears. A low voice works its way up from inside me, Vulstus's voice, speaking to me in our ancient tongue.

"What other secrets do you hold, Aestrangel?" he says, and I can feel him scanning me from the inside.

I stiffen up, protecting myself, protecting the secret of Apophis and my true inner power. "I told you; a sword and shield will do me no good," I say out loud with a strong, firm voice.

"They will serve you well on the battlefield. With your wings still in formation, you have no other choice."

I stare straight ahead, daring not to protest any further. "Thank you, Vulstus. I will put them to good use."

He nods again. "Go now. Practice. And when you return, your army will be ready for you," he says, and he releases his hands from the skulls.

I leave and make my way to the entryway of Gehenna. I stand atop one of the craggy hills with the Lake of Fire beneath me and the passageway to the world above. A hollow wind from below tangles my hair into a frenzied mass, and my vision is blurred. Without wings, I'm not sure how I will make it above. Without wings, I'm not sure how I will survive the fall below. I get down on my knees and rack my brain, thinking of my options and coming away empty-handed when the snake inside me twitches, jolts me up an inch off the ground, and I get an idea.

I rise up to one knee and stake my sword in the ground beside me. I encase myself in golden light and let the energy fill me, lift me, give me a sort of weightlessness as if the light itself had wings. Holding on to the hilt, I cata-pult my body upward, and I am airborne! I race through the precipice like a flash of light emerging from the depths of the Earth. I am the shooting star up from the darkness of the hellfire! The very opposite of the Angels' descent from The Observatory. I am risen.

And when I get to Earth, there is no stopping my wrath. There is no Calling to help and nurture. There is no fake human life to succumb to. Just me. Full of steel, power, glory, and vengeance—armored with the souls of the damned, powered by my own will and the evil of my brethren.

*And I do so beget evil upon the land.*

I hurl myself across the globe, to every corner of the human world, and brandish my sword so artistically that to the human eye, they have no idea I am even coming. I strike down upon them with such cataclysmic fury that in mere seconds I have induced misery and destruction by the score. For me, it happens in all but a moment, a short fraction of time, but for them, their torment will echo for ages.

Their blood invigorates me. I am covered in it. Armor stained from head to toe in dark brown gore.

Their screams intoxicate me. I am drunk with energy. I am high, helpless with power. Apophis suckles the sensations from the inside and stretches its arms within, absorbing the souls of my human victims. My skin, no longer white with purity, becomes a hazed iridescent gray, making room for my weapon to grow stronger still.

When I am finished, when I have tasted enough, when I have readied myself to lead and command, I return to the precipice of Gehenna and look down below. My army is waiting for me. Thousands upon thousands of demons of all orders are suited and lined up—waiting for my command, waiting for my direction. They witnessed my carnage on Earth and took the initiative to be prepared for my return. Row after row, they stand at attention, face forward, weapons in hand, ready and willing to obey like

Vulstus said they would. My heart swells with pride, and for a moment, I wish Malek was here by my side.

*If this is what it feels like to rule...*

My torture and torment, isolation, and manipulation have brought me to this moment. I am one step closer to my ultimate goal of domination. The blood of the people is still warm and wet on my face. I wipe my brow with the back of one hand and stab my sword into the ground with the other. "Daimones!" I cry out to the denizens below, and at once, they stamp their weapons on the ground, shaking the very foundation of the cave.

"I have infected the lands of the people. Ravaged them with famine and disease. Laid waste to their cities. I have turned brother from brother and driven them to murder. I have ripped screaming children straight from their mothers' arms. I have made them recognize that we are a true and present danger in their lives, and we deserve respect and offerings just as much as the one above us. Not only I have done these things to show our power and glory, but I have also done these things in service to our Lord—the Dark God who walks among his subjects, not some mysterious being hidden in clouds and smoke.

"Now, I have chosen you to rise with me!" I scream. I pull my sword from the ground and raise it high over my head. Blood and gore drip from the blade and onto my face. My tongue laps at my lips for a taste of the sweet honey. "To defeat our enemies! To cast them out and away like they did to our brethren eons ago!"

The demon soldiers raise their weapons simultaneously and in unison utter a battle cry—a dissonant sound of agony and pleasure.

"For we are Legion! All and nothing. Many and none. We are Legion! And failure is not an option."

# THE GREAT WAR

A trumpet sounds in the distance, and all demons before me stand at attention. It is the herald cry of Pursan, the daimon with the body of a human and the face of a lion. He rides atop a rabid bear and controls his beast with reins made of deadly vipers. His task is to blow his trumpet when there is news to be spread throughout Gehenna. He is Lucifer's messenger, and when the trumpet sounds, all below take heed. I look over my army with pride once more before crouching down low and springing up on my legs and soaring through the air above the cavern. I know the hour is close at hand—the hour of the War between the Angelos and the Daimones. Pursan's musical alert lets us all know we are on the edge of battle.

All the important officers are assembled in the throne room, and I make my way to my appointed seat next to Lucifer. Malek is present. He is outfitted in similar armor to me, and when our eyes meet, he sweeps a glancing look over my new garb and bows his head with an approving nod. I return the gesture and smile in spite of myself. I can't help but feel a quivering rush when I'm around him. I can't help but keep my eyes locked on his in a lustful stare-down.

Lucifer clears his throat and raises his arm in the air. "What news do you have to share?" he says to Malek.

Malek takes a step forward and runs a hand down the front of his red and gold breastplate. His golden winged helmet is nestled in the crook of his arm. "I've consulted, at length, with some of the Watchers, and after much deliberation, they've agreed to meet on the Astral Plane."

"To meet?" Lucifer questions, which strikes me odd that he would question that. If the Angelos are not interested in fighting, it would make sense that they would want to convene on neutral ground. I remember the stories about the aftermath of the first war between the Angelos and Daimones in Ilarium. After the Lord cast Lucifer and the others out, it was said that they met frequently on the Astral Plane working out the guidelines of the "new reality" that had been created. Because Lucifer was no longer allowed in Ilarium, and the Creator had no desire to traverse to Gehenna, the Astral Plane was formed as a neutral zone where both sides could meet to conduct any business necessary. There was to be no fighting, or tricks, or bloodshed in this realm. It was also said that the creator, in all his infinite wisdom, still tried to persuade the Morning Star to reconsider his new path and come back to the order of the Seraphim, but Lucifer denied the almighty time and time again. *After* the war, *after* all the death and destruction and betrayal, the creator was still willing to forgive Lucifer and turn things around. But that is merely one side of the story—the version I was fed when I was an angel. And as I have grown in my strange nature, I have learned there are two sides to every story, and then there's the truth. Ask Angelos, and they will tell you they won the war. Ask the Daimones, and they will tell you they won the war.

*What truth will be left when all of* this *is said and done?*

Malek clears his throat with the same haunting timbre of his father. "Yes," he continues. "They don't want to fight. They want to avoid war at all costs. They hope that we can all come to some form of agreement. A bargain, if you will."

Lucifer rubs his smooth stone-like chin with his long fingers, brooding over the possibilities. "They want something," he mutters to himself, and the silly human girl in me wants to automatically respond, "Duh," but I literally bite my tongue to prevent the obnoxious noise from escaping my lips and let my mouth fill with my own deliciously sweet blood. The distressed look on his face tells the entire room that he is at a loss for what their motives truly are. "I don't trust it," he finally says loudly in the language of the ancients. The throne room shakes at the sound of his voice, and Lilith shudders in her corner. "There has to be more to it," he continues, "and so yes, we will meet with them on neutral territory, but we will not come empty handed."

"We will be ready for whatever is to come, Father," Malek says in his best General voice.

"No," Lucifer responds. "I will need you here in Gehenna. Aestrangel will accompany me to the Astral Plane along with her masses. You need to be here to protect Lilith and Alukah and this realm if anything were to transpire out there. I will need you, Malek, to act in my stead if we are attacked or need to mobilize. Your legions will remain here with you should the need arise. You will follow the call to lead them to fight. But for this—for this initial summit, I want you here."

On the surface, it sounds so pretty. Malek in charge of Gehenna while Daddy is away on business. But there is a condescending bite in the Prince of Darkness's tone that lets everyone in the room know it is somewhat of a back-handed compliment. The color from Malek's face drains, but he retains his composure and bows in agreement to the Morning Star.

Lucifer stands up, and in a flash, his aura has reached a black fever-pitch. He makes a semi-circle motion on the floor in front of him and turns to me. "Wherever your army is, they will follow. Thousands of them. Thousands upon thousands at your command. You will serve me well, young one."

The ground rumbles and shakes and a gaping hole forms before us. Smoke rises from beneath and in a great tumult, my body is being pulled by an invisible magnet. I struggle to see Malek, to locate where he is in the room, to bid him farewell and good luck, to let him know my love for him is strong and deep and wide and complete, but the images around me are hazy, fuzzy, out of focus. Lucifer recites an old spell in the ancient tongue, the hole in the ground swallows us both, and I slip deep into the great chasm of blackness.

—✕—✕—✳—✕—✕—

The Astral Plane is a wondrous void. An open field of nothing. It's not like Asphodel where my inner thoughts and desires are scanned and manipulated. It's not peaceful, nor does it fill my heart with love like Ilarium. And it certainly isn't a heavy weight on my soul like Gehenna. It is a great field of neutrality set among a black night sky. Millions of stars twinkle around us, and I wonder if they are the army of Angelos lying in wait, ready and poised to strike. But they wouldn't begin a battle in this place that was designed to be a safe harbor... would they?

I stand behind and to the left of the Morning Star. The blade of my sword is covered in its sheath at my hip, but my hand is firmly on the hilt, ready for Lucifer's signal should he deem it necessary to attack. Metal clanks and clashes behind me, and I glance over my shoulder to see that one by one, my army appears—a great mass of twisted, armored warrior-demons trained to follow my command.

Soon, the stars illuminate more brightly. Some of them grow and bend and drop out of the sky like giant raindrops. They glow when they fall to the ground and suddenly transform into their chosen shapes. The Archangel Michael, the head of the Seraphim and the creator's greatest warrior, manifests first. He has six wings that breathe pure fire, and in all the years I was in Ilarium, this is the first time I have ever been in his infernal presence. Behind Michael, Drakonas, the Dominion with the booming voice, manifests from his oversized raindrop. Then Uriah, the Ophanim who represents the Wheel of Fate, arises. Following him, the angel lovers Revalia and Lozhure appear. Revalia—my former sister-angel, the one angelic soul who spoke to mine when we were in Ilarium. She forms so beautifully from her astral pod—her long brown hair sweeps over her milky white shoulders as she fans out her violet-colored wings, as if she's shaking them out and waking herself up from a long and dreamless slumber. I remember my love for her was boundless and weightless and never-ending until she failed her first Calling and fell under the spell of the failed angel Lozhure. I remember that Camael had told me Revalia and Lozhure would never be able to move up in the Angelic Order because of their transgressions as humans on Earth. It's puzzling that The Powers That Be would allow two grunts in their order to accompany the high-ranking angels on a mission such as this.

Lucifer inhales deeply as the angels approach. His exhale swirls around us with a calming mist. Michael leads his angels to meet us, but they stop, frozen, about ten feet away. A magnetic hum fills my ears as the atmosphere in the Astral Plane feels weighted down and dry. All angel eyes are fixated on me, even the millions upon millions in Uriah's wheel. Their irises are like tiny purple flowers, familiar to my astral gene. Looking at them awakens something in me, like I'm trying to remember something but can't. Revalia's mouth is wide open in shock when she sees me, and the angels do not speak a word. But I can hear them. I can hear the wave of their voices passing back and forth to each other in the ether in a language that I know I once knew but can no longer decipher. Their voices are rushed and frantic and fill me with suspicion. I look at Lucifer and scan his face, wondering if he too can hear their conversation, but there is no indication that he can. Apophis stirs on my insides as I sense the angels trying to scan me, trying to work their way inside my soul to have a glimpse or take a taste. Hundreds of ethereal hands grab for my essence and try clawing their way inside. Apophis pushes back—it struggles and wrestles with its prying claws, and it lurches me forward uncontrollably. I stumble a step until it gives one last strangle and quiets down, and then it hits me—I had completely forgotten about Camael. I have not heard his voice in what feels like forever, but he must still be here with me, and they sense him.

The angel voices stop flittering and Michael, glorious flame-enshrouded Michael, steps forward to come face to face with the Morning Star.

"Sweet Michael," Lucifer says in a sing-songy voice. "Burning with a passion for our father. Ignited with a fiery love that is all consuming. You look well, brother. Did I look that beautiful when I held the rank of Seraphim?" he jokes.

The angels stare blankly at him.

"I'm surprised he sent you," he continues coyly. "I thought you wanted peace."

"We do," Michael says, and his voice is melodic and fills the Astral Plane with a vibration of a choral song.

"Ah yes, but you are the Enforcer, are you not? We always struggled for his attention, didn't we? I thought the peace loving Selaphiel or Metatron would have been dispatched, but you? The last time we met..."

"No good came from it."

Lucifer chuckles. "That's a matter of opinion, dear Michael. I beg to differ. But we're certainly not here to play catch-up and reminisce about the past, are we?"

A fireball shoots up from Michael's wings. "Of course not," he says.

"Speak your terms then. I wait with bated breath to hear what you could possibly want from..."

"Aestra. We are here for her."

It takes a second for it to register in my mind.

*Me. They are talking about me.*

He speaks of me with the name I have buried so long ago. A name that isn't even familiar to my own ears. My body stiffens. My metal armor clanks at my side. Lucifer glances over at me and narrows his brow. "Aestrangel? And what would you need her for?" he asks, rubbing his temple.

Michael fans out his wings and a wave of yellow and orange light surrounds him. "Whatever name you have given her is of no matter to us. She is to be judged—punished for her crimes against the holy host and against humanity itself."

"And how do you suggest you are going to accomplish that?"

Drakonas steps forward from behind Michael. "Aestra is to come to Ilarium with us," he pronounces, and his voice booms in the Astral Plane as I remember. "For what greater punishment for a daimon than to be in the ever-consuming presence of the Lord?"

A part of me fears Lucifer will turn me over to them, and yet another part of me is thrilled at the prospect of them trying to subdue me. I keep my composure and remain silent.

"How interestingly ironic," the Morning Star coos. "You plan on carving out a little slice of Hell in your perfect paradise."

"Camael was murdered on holy ground," Michael says. "The rules have changed. Aestra must make penance for what she's done. In our care, she will no longer be able to do harm to anyone or anything else."

Lucifer steps forward into the space between them and turns his back on Michael. He looks at me lovingly, fondly. He extends his arm in my direction, and I reach for his hand. I keep his gaze. I don't break it. I scan his black eyes for meaning and substance. I scan his face for an answer to a riddle, but I already know the answer. I already know his loyalty lies with me. "What makes you think I would do that? What makes you think I would allow that to happen? What makes you think I would turn over one of my most precious acolytes?"

He brings my hand to his lips for an icy kiss. His cold aura shivers against my armor and engulfs my entire body in a chill all the way to my core, and my breath becomes visible when I exhale. Lucifer gives me a sly smile, releases my hand, and turns back to Michael and the angels. "And what if I agree? What if I say, 'Fine, have her?' What's in it for me? What's my 'finder's fee,' so to speak?"

"If you return her to us, we give our God-ruled word that there will be no battle. No bloodshed. No war." Michael says calmly, but I can tell from his voice he is becoming more and more agitated.

"Oh, brother," Lucifer says with a *tsk*. "Surely, that is not going to be enough. You know what I want."

Michael pauses and the two engage in a lengthy stare. Much has happened between them over the ages, and Michael looks upon the Morning Star with an expression of undeniable concern. Like an older brother who cannot condone the actions of his sibling. He sighs heavily. "And you know that will never happen."

*Property? Are they bartering for me like a piece of property?* Like a thing that can be traded or sold in the name of peace or for some other demand to check off Lucifer's list? I feel sick at this exchange.

"You know, brother, it never fails to amaze me that the almighty, the all-seeing, the all-knowing, would allow me to influence and do such terrible things to his beloved creation when all it would take is..."

I sense my army shift and stir behind me, so I instinctively tighten my grip on the hilt of my sword.

"It's not going to happen!" Michael reiterates, raising his voice. "She doesn't belong to you!"

"Nor does she belong to you!" Lucifer roars in my defense, and my heart lightens at his assertion. "I think Aestrangel has chosen for herself which side she'd rather be on."

"Actually, Sataniel, that's where *we* beg to differ."

I look at Revalia who stares at me with a pained expression. I try to figure out her thoughts, her emotions, but she's closed off to me—an ancient puzzle from long ago.

"A piece of Camael still lives inside Aestra," Drakonas says, "and he needs to come home. To be reincorporated with the breath of the Creator."

That's what they were sensing. That's why they groped and scratched at me. That's why my newfound power shut them down.

Lucifer's eyebrows rise in delight and excitement.

"Ideally, you will come with us of your own free will," Revalia interjects and speaks directly to me.

I now know why they sent her. They had hoped she would be able to tap into that part of me that had loved her just as much. They had hoped she would be able to awaken and ignite my angelic sense of moral right.

Lucifer puts a hand on my shoulder. "You must be very special to them," he whispers. "Look at all the trouble they are going through. Just. For. You."

I am not fazed by his words.

"Aestra, please," Revalia pleads. "If there's any part of you that is still angel, any part of you that still remembers, any part of you that still feels, you'll do the right thing. Come with us. Bring Camael home. Let him rest. He loved you so. *I* love you so."

Her voice is like a hollow bell in my head. Her words are meaningless to me. Any love and affection I once felt for her is gone. Erased. I try to search my mind and heart for any nostalgic feeling from my past—from our past—and all I can conjure are feelings of resentment, abandonment, loneliness, and shame. Lozhure standing next to her doesn't help much either. I remember how he treated me in The Observatory. How he forced me to do something once that was against everything I stood for. Revalia's voice only makes me irritated and angry. She is nothing to me. She means nothing to me.

I withdraw my sword.

*Sorry, Revalia, but you've failed yet again.*

I grasp my sword with both hands and stand sideways and firm with my feet planted in the astral soil.

Lucifer's eyes widen at my posture. "Well, Michael, I believe we have our answer."

"It doesn't have to be this way," he says, his wings flapping uncontrollably.

"Apparently, it does," Lucifer says, and the legion behind me cries out with a deep war cry of "hoo-rah."

"We tried to make peace," Michael says as he begins to drift upward in the air. The angels in his group follow his lead. "This is on you."

"It's always about me," Lucifer says with a smile, and I raise my sword in the air. "Just this time it's about her too."

"It's more than that, and you know it."

Lucifer shrugs his shoulders. "Perhaps. We will soon find out, won't we?"

"Yes. Oh, yes we will."

CHAPTER ELEVEN

# THE GREAT WAR (PART 2)

Against the dark sky, against the milky white stars, something like a smile snakes across Lucifer's face. I hold my breath, brandish my sword high above me, and wait for his signal. I have thousands at my back—so many that I'm not even sure of the actual count. Lucifer screams "Hold!" to us all telepathically, and the army stamps a collective foot on the ground in acknowledgment.

Michael and the other angels take a bent knee, on the ground, spread their wings at their sides, and bow their heads in prayer. Is it their final prayer to the creator? Is it a prayer of penance for failing to obtain me? Is it a goodbye? It must be because they are certainly no match for us. This will be an easy fight—me, Lucifer, and my legions versus the five before us. My sword will strike swiftly, and we can be back in Gehenna in no time.

*But it can't be this easy. Nothing is this easy.*

Uriah, the Wheel, opens every eye on every spoke, and they sing out in a chorus, quoting the human's holy book, recounting the tale of their first deadly encounter on sacred land: "Then war broke out in heaven. Michael and his angels fought against the demon, and the demon and his angels fought back. But he was not strong enough, and they lost their place in heaven. The great demon was hurled down—that ancient serpent called the devil, or Sataniel, who leads the whole world astray. He was hurled to the Earth and his angels with him."

Lucifer laughs, but I can't tell if it is proud laughter or one of doubt. Maybe it's a little of both. When Lucifer was cast out, he essentially had gotten what he wanted, thus warping his perception of the battle as a win for him. But perhaps the memory still stings in him. Perhaps it still bites away at him because I know there is something that Lucifer still wants from the creator. Something he has yet to achieve. And I have a feeling there is doubt in that chuckle. Doubt that he will be successful in getting what his heart desires.

Suddenly, a great rush and tumult shakes from the sky in the form of rolling thunder as dark gray clouds race across the horizon. Lucifer takes pause and surveys the sky. In an instant, he unfurls his black wings that he so craftily keeps hidden and takes his place at the front of our battle line. A swirling cyclone of glittering beams dances around him, and he transforms, revealing his true demonic nature.

"What's happening?" I shout to him above the roar of the thunder.

"It's begun, Aestrangel. Ready yourself. They are coming for you. You and you alone are their one true objective. Guide your masses to protect you at all costs.

Hide amongst them if you must." He is huge now—a monstrous being standing on hind legs with cloven hooves and studded horns like thick Ibex antlers spiraling from the sides of his head.

Hide? That's not what Generals do. It strikes me odd that he would instruct me to act so cowardly, but I take his command to heart. He is trying to protect me. He wants to keep me safe.

"I'm here to fight!" I assert. "I'm here beside you ready to win this war! And look, it's just the five of them!"

"It won't be for long." With his gigantic, clawed finger, he points to the horizon where the gray clouds have dissipated. I look, and in the distance, the stars start to fall—one by one, star by star, like a meteor shower filling the sky. They burn and glisten and fizzle and hit the ground, like Michael and the others did. Like raindrops plopping open and evaporating into thin air.

But only, they don't evaporate.

Every single one of them is an angel. Descended, shaken off, armed, ready. I know they are equipped with their holy host! They are beautiful! A glowing mass of glorious power shining their way across the field—hypnotizing me as they advance toward us. I can't take my eyes off them as I watch them fall, awaken, collect themselves, configure together, and move steadily forward for battle in a mass of fluid light that emanates the energy of the purest love.

I knew this wasn't going to be easy.

Lucifer pushes me back into the first line of my legion, like he's trying to camouflage me amongst them. "Use whatever charms you have. Take down as many as you can. Stay safe. Stay alive. Without your wings, you will need to be crafty. Be crafty," he says, and he takes to the sky. The gust of wind from his wingspan breaks me from my semi-trance, and I sulk between the armed shoulders of my men.

"Wait for it!" I scream to them in my mind.

"Protect the Dark Star!" Lucifer responds to us all internally.

I creep further and further, deep into the masses, hiding myself among monster and steel. "Wait for it!" I repeat, and they hold their weapons steady, anxiously waiting for my command.

Above us, Lucifer soars upward to meet Michael in the air. The jet-black feathers on his massive wings shimmer with the hue of an oil slick—greens, purples, and golds catch the light of the angels and make him sparkle as he ascends closer to his adversary. Michael is in full fiery rage—as enormous as the Dark Lord and engulfed in the holiest of flames that even his eyes burn with tiny orange blazes. Their colossal bodies clash mid-air with a thunderous bang to start the combat on the ground.

"Now!" I scream out loud to my militia, and they go tearing off to attack.

And I slink back even farther behind them.

The clanking and clanging of swords against shields against armory against astral forces reverberates in the Astral Plane, deafens my ears, and fills me with a flash of excitement. Yes! I want to join the fray! I want to run my sword deep into the belly of a Guardian Angel. I want to snuff out the light of my former kin. I want to bathe myself in the dying life-force of a screaming cherub.

But I hide.

*Like a coward.*

And I cower.

*Like someone who is helpless and weak.*

In the distance, flashes of lightning strike the soil. "Push forward!" I mentally command my crew, and the line in front of me takes a step forward.

And I move a step behind, sinking among my denizens. Lost and frightened in my own mind. Anxiously holding on to the hope that this will soon be over, and I can go back to Gehenna. I cannot let them take me to Ilarium. I cannot let them...

Then a wicked thought creeps into my head. Maybe this is what Lucifer wanted all along. He wanted me to create a child to infiltrate The Observatory, but when that obviously was not going to happen, maybe the prospect of me being remanded to the heavens is the next best thing for him? Maybe this battle is a precursor of what's to come? Maybe the true battle starts when I try to claw my way out of Ilarium? Were his instructions for me to hide a means to an end?

I shake my head, trying to rid myself of the thought. Lucifer's actions and intentions are usually literally aligned. Literally. I've come to learn that there's always a double meaning, a double-edged sword, open for inter-pretation. *His interpretation*. For what he says is Law in his domain.

The next line of my army pushes ahead. The battle is evenly matched as I can see flickers of lights dying away as angels fall, and clutches of my slain troops piled on top of each other. My heart aches for I am not in the midst of it. What kind of leader am I if I am not fighting alongside those who have sworn allegiance to me? I crouch down low and whisper to Apophis. Lucifer was right—without my wings, my power is limited, but I have my steel. And my strength. And my guiles. I form a barrier around me in my astral mind—a golden haze of protection that I know will only last temporarily, and I stand and wade through my warriors, inching my way back to the front of the line … where I belong. Like Moses parting the Red Sea, my soldiers stop to look at me, puzzled, before they step aside. There is confusion in their gestures and facial expressions. They had been instructed to protect me at all costs, and they are to follow my every instruction, yet now those two directives are in direct conflict with each other, and it leaves them jarred and unsure. "No worries," I say to them in my mind. "Keep pushing ahead." They step aside to let me through, and once I pass with my golden aura, they continue on.

When I reach the front of the line, when the massacre comes into full view, I am tantalized. Husks of bodies from both sides litter the realm, and I am refreshed with a sense of duty. This is my fight. My battle. The angels kept at my warriors, trying to whittle them down and break through their bastion so they could ultimately collect me. But here I am—in full sight, and as my actions confused my own soldiers, the angel warriors are just as perplexed.

Like Lucifer said, I must be crafty, because I can feel the golden barrier around me start to weaken. I kneel down on one knee and caress the ground beneath me. I pet it, speak to it, whisper words of love and affection. And an apology. I can bend the soil to do my will because of our long history together. She remembers me—remembers when I seeped into her core and destroyed her soul. And she forgives me, like all parents do for their children, no matter the offense. As a child of above and below and between, I have dominion overall. I am Aestrangel! The strangest of them all! The strongest of them all!

Crunching claws and microscopic teeth scrape against the ground beneath me as a blanket of ethereal stag beetles rise from the earth and race across the plain. They are attracted to the light of the holy host and are eager to attack. With their charmed pinchers, they nip at the feet and ankles of my opponents, climb their way up their astral bodies, and puncture holes in their astral selves. Their lights start to ooze out of their wounds as they moan piteously on the field.

Lucifer and Michael continue their confrontation in the sky, but the Morning Star is distracted by my insect attack and looks down unapprovingly right before Michael is able to land a fiery blow to the side of his face. At that instant, the golden barrier around me melts away, and I am left open to the angels' fury. My warriors surround me to provide protection, but I unsheathe my sword and rush into the line hacking and slashing at everything and anything in my path—my own fighters included.

One by one, I take them down—with circular motions, with stabbing motions, with ripping and tearing and decapitating motions. It is a frenzied furor, a berserker's dream of hacking and slashing, mutilating, and piercing…

*…and rejuvenating.*

Because I've done this before. Every soul of my felled enemy, every soul of my felled comrade is fed into mine. I dance across the arena, weave in and out of the downed combatants from both sides and inhale them, breathe them into me. With each one I slay and consume, I am filled with a maddening flood of energy. Astral inebriation at its finest! A drunken carnival of slay and ingest. They are all with me now.

The metal studs on my back twitch and tingle, and I know my wings are strengthening with each spirit I absorb, but Apophis stretches its arms inside me, and it drops me to my knees with a blast of searing hot pain. I'm on fire on the inside, perhaps from the overindulgence of energy. My sword falls to my side, and the warriors quickly huddle over me—the drones protecting the queen in the hive. The cacophony of battle is muffled as their bodies stifle every sound out. It's as if my head is submerged underwater, but as each second passes, the noises become clearer, more defined, more acute. I suddenly realize that my warriors, in their unwavering loyalty to protect me, are not protecting themselves, and one by one, an angel attack is slicing them open and flinging their demon bodies atop a pile beside me.

Soon, I am no longer protected. I look up from my kneeled position and glance at the stinking heap of my dead—bloodied suits of armor no longer able to shield the quickly decaying shells inside them. Demon bodies still burn from inside their metal chain mails—the stench of their blistering and scorched flesh wafting in the circle of air around them. I reach for my sword on the ground and rise. A blinding light forces me to cup a hand over my brow to protect my eyes. I squint. I try to focus. A figure materializes from the strong glow, and the light dims a little. Finally, when my eyes adjust, I see the angel before me.

"Oh, *you*," I huff.

## CHAPTER TWELVE

# THE VICTOR

Lozhure turns down his light, and I lower my hand from my face and tighten the grip on my sword. His aura is muted to a dark navy blue—a comforting color of peace and tranquility, and his wings are folded behind him in a non-threatening way. He extends his long arm out with his palm faced down and makes a stroking gesture like a circus trainer trying to calm a wild animal. I nearly choke on a laugh. *He* thinks he can quiet *me*? As far as I'm concerned, he should be on his knees worshipping the ground I allow him to walk on.

He gingerly approaches me. "Aestra," he says in a steady voice. "It's ok, Aestra. No one wants to hurt you."

I narrow my eyes and tilt my head to the side.

"It's over. It's all over. The Daimones have fled or fallen. You're going to come with me now."

I look over my shoulder, and yes, I am alone. My militia no longer backs me up. I stand on the line in solitude. But what he says isn't true. The war still rages deep on the battlefield. I see the engagement in full effect on the horizon. Lucifer still tangles in the sky with Michael in their evenly-matched dance. "I'm not going anywhere with you," I growl and twirl the blade of my sword into the ground.

For a quick second, his aura flashes with aggravated purple, and with his free hand, he runs his fingers through his long brown hair. Such a human thing to do, yet it doesn't surprise me because of all of the Angelos, Lozhure and Revalia are the most human. His brown locks shimmer like silk in the sunlight, like dead fish glittering along the sea. His hair reminds me of beauty and brutality.

I turn sideways in a defensive stance.

"We don't want anyone else to get hurt," he says gently. "There's been enough bloodshed on both sides. Look," he points to the field behind me.

Instinctively, I turn my head again as his voice trails in my memory...

*Just look! It's so wonderful.*

Remembering those words, remembering his voice, remembering what he did to me...

I always knew there was something about Lozhure—something *in* Lozhure—that didn't speak to my astral self. The night he forced me in The Observatory, and I caught a forbidden glimpse of my Calling, he had held my arms behind my back, overpowered me like I was a weak nothing. I was weak back then—weak in mind and weak in spirit, never questioning the ways of our kind or even the world around us. I had blind faith—steadfast and never wavering, and my love of the Lord and all his creations was innocent, and pure, and true. Lozhure used my good-natured essence against me. He preyed upon my weakness and tricked me into sin. And then again, in the human realm, he attacked me from behind, pinned me, gagged me, and forced me to meet with the Watcher. I was still new then, too, just in the beginning stages of flexing my demonic muscle, still growing and in the process of shedding my angelic skin. He used my transitioning period against me, using tools of his human design and the power of his human strength to subdue me. He put me into a hold of submission and forced me to complete his task.

Twice he has gotten the best of me.

*There will not be a third.*

Slowly, I turn my head back around and raise my sword to waist level. "I said, I'm not going anywhere with you," I say through gritted teeth.

He moves to the side in a questionable way. My senses are piqued at his movement, and my eyes are trained on his every step. Is he trying to get behind me? Does he think he can creep up on me again and pin me like he's done in the past? "Be reasonable. We're your family. You were born of the Creator, just like me, like Revalia, like Camael."

Even his words are suspect, and I find myself moving in a semi-circle, following him intently. "Family?" I laugh.

"It's going to be okay," he says as he makes a move toward me.

Without thinking, I pull back my arms and bury my sword in the center of his throat. He gurgles and twitches and uses both of his hands to grasp at the weapon to try to pull it free. His eyes blink uncontrollably, and he's been human so many times, that there's actual blood— red, thin, warm—spraying out in a gentle mist from the wound. He chokes on a mixture of his human fluids and his astral light. It bubbles up, collects on his tongue, and begins leaking out the sides of his mouth. My blade has gone straight through him, and it captures his blue light, sucks it up into the steel, and slides down in electric waves into my hands and up my arms until Lozhure permeates my whole body. He convulses as I draw his essence into me, and I smile knowing I have gotten my revenge.

*Who's the weak one now?* I think as I withdraw my sword. And I smile, knowing he can never hurt me again.

Revalia screams a heart-wrenching wail of loss and pain that echoes across the Plane. The agony of her dirge is a cacophony of ungodly noises beyond any of the wailing I've heard in the Halls of Punishment. The death of Lozhure penetrates her even more deeply than the death of Camael for Lozhure was her companion, her soulmate, her love, and his vicious demise shakes her to the very core—brings her to the darkest place of supreme misery and ultimate despair. A part of me empathizes with her pain—I briefly imagine if it were *me* witnessing the death of Malek. What guttural sounds would emit from *my* chest?

In a flash, she crashes to the ground to be by his side. She shakes him through her tears and yells at him to "Look at me! Wake up! Stop playing around! Don't leave me now! Don't leave me like this!" All human pre-programmed phrases for the meat-shells to dispense when they are faced with a sudden, traumatic loss. She cradles him lovingly in her arms as the last of his light flickers off. Her hot, human tears can't save him, nor can her mystical, angelic ones.

"What have you done?" she screams at me.

I'm still reeling from Lozhure entering me as Apophis shifts and stumbles inside trying to make room for yet another influx of energy. She confuses my silence for sympathy, but really I'm unsteady on my feet, shifting my weight back and forth from foot to foot, trying to catch my balance. Lozhure's power rocked me! My head swims as I try to regain my composure and situational awareness.

Revalia gently rests Lozhure's lifeless body down and rises. Her purple wings extend at her sides, and she is illuminated with a soft glow. She looks spectacular! Breathtaking. Awe-inspiring. She has never been this radiant before. My head swims again, and I feel like I'm losing myself in her moment, in her presence, but I am Aestrangel—adjusting to my new body, shifting with my new power.

*I am Aestrangel. I am Aestrangel.* I repeat to myself, over and over. I command Apophis to take up the mantra, and it too, shouts the words from inside.

"Aestra!" she gushes, and her smile opens a box of memories inside of me. "Sister!" she exclaims, and she rushes over to me. Her human-like arms wrap around my neck as she engulfs the rest of me in her violet wings. The feather tips graze along my newly budding stumps and the sensation of an angel kiss sends shivers down my back. She is familiar. She is new. Yet she is old. And comforting. In my confusion, my arm reaches up over her feathers and caresses the quills lovingly. I remember her softness, and her sadness, and my need to help and save her from Lozhure and herself. Is she now thanking me for snuffing out his light? Is she thanking me for cutting him out of her life? When she is this close to me, can she feel him racing through my astral veins? She and I have always been bonded together, always sharing a special con-nection. From the beginning of my existence, there has always been Revalia, so sayeth the Lord. Sweet, brown-haired, purple-souled Revalia. My angel sister.

*Aestra...* I know that name. Isn't that my name?

No, that can't be right.

*I am Aestrangel. I am Aestrangel...*

"Revalia?" I mutter.

She steps back and holds me at arm's length. "Oh, my dear! Oh, my love!"

I smell a heavy scent of flowers burning—it's a pungent smell, if burnt orchid and lavender mixed with a hint of melting copper. I look down at my body armor and notice a section of my breastplate has melted away exposing a small section of my bare torso. I shake my head to bring myself back into focus.

"What's happening, Revalia? Are you really here?"

"Yes, Aestra, I'm here. We're on the Astral Plane. The war is over. You're coming home with me." She smiles and flashes a vibrant, pale violet hue. I remember our home together—the simulated apartment constructed by the Powers That Be to train us in our human ways. We lived together, laughed together, told each other our wildest dreams and fears. I remember her cooking at the human stovetop each morning and singing with her glorious angel voice. Oh, the songs, the heavenly songs she sang were enough to lull me to the ninth realm!

I swipe madly at my shoulder. A sensation like fire ant bites smarts my flesh, and when I look down, I notice more iron on my armor has melted away. Explosions blare from the sky, and I look up to see the fiery war raging in full force above me. "Home?" I stupidly question.

She smiles again. "Yes, home, Aestra! Home—where we will be happy and safe. We're going to bring Lozhure there, and Camael too."

"Lozhure?" I repeat, dumbfounded. "But Lozhure's dead. And so is Camael. I... I killed them both. I... I killed..."

My voice trails off as another explosion booms close by, and Michael continues to rain down a firestorm around us. She still smiles at me, but there's a glint in her eye that gives her fear away. She's afraid of me. I might not be able to read her thoughts, but I can tell this much by the subtle strobe in her eyes and the delicate tremor of her extended feathers.

"Stop denying your true nature and come home with me, Aestra. We'll sort everything out when we get back to Ilarium."

Screams in the distance snap me back to reality, and I spit her words back at her. "Denying my true nature? Living in Ilarium was denying my true nature." I extend my arms to my sides. "*This* is my true nature," I declare and slam the blade of my sword against my chest. She jolts at the sound of the crashing metal. "You are nothing but a slave, only you're taught to believe you're doing something good and worthy."

Her aura dances stronger around her with a protective rhythm. "And you're not? You're not a slave to the Prince of Lies?"

"I make my own choices. I have true free will."

She lowers her head apologetically, and her shoulders slump slightly downward. "Oh, Aestra. That's not what I've heard. What has he done to you? What has he let happen to you? Let me help you. Let us help you. The Lord will forgive all your transgressions, you know?"

How dare she pretend to know me! To know what I've gone through! To know what goes on in my mind! "The hypocrisy of the righteous never fails to amaze me."

"Your anger runs so deep, I know. But there must be a piece of you left that remembers the all-encompassing love of the Creator. There must be a piece of you left that remembers the unconditional love I gave you." She bats her eyes as she tries to plead with me.

"No," I lie. "I feel nothing... nothing for you, nothing for him, nothing for the place you call home."

"I don't believe you!" she scoffs. "We were bonded at creation. And you are always here with me," she points to the center of her chest. "I will always carry your memory with me. Every conversation we ever had. Every angelic kiss of our wings. You are always here, inside of me. Always in my reach. I can call to you in my dreams, and bring you back to the way things used to be in my memories, Aestra."

I nudge Lozhure's lifeless body with my sword, and I remember his betrayal. I remember *her* betrayal. She never stopped him. She never helped me. She called me weak and conspired against me. She conspires against me still. She doesn't deserve to keep my memory with her. She doesn't deserve to have my name dance upon her tongue, even if in a dream. She doesn't deserve to have the mere knowledge of my existence in her mind and in her heart. I want to take it from her and make them mine again. She doesn't get to carry around what used to be. She shouldn't be allowed to hold on to the name of *Aestra*. I am not Aestra. Aestra is no more.

*I am Aestrangel.*

"Where do you keep me?" I ask her after a moment of feigned hesitation. "Where do you keep my memory?"

Her purple aura flutters with happiness and delight, like she's gotten through to me. "Here, sweet sister." She rubs the astral skin on her chest in a circular motion and a web of interchanging colors blossoms across the surface. Each line of the spidery image interlocks and overlaps and interconnects, each delicate thread a physical manifestation of her recollections.

"There? Beneath your surface?" I ask.

"Yes," she says, and she blushes a pink hue. "I created this to hold you together. So I wouldn't forget."

Its complexity fascinates me as I study the image more closely. The silky thread runs deep inside of her, all the way to the underbelly of her astral core. And I think, *Is this what she was built for? Designed to preserve the memory of Aestra? Was this the creator's ultimate intention?*

I extend my hand. "May I?" I ask, attempting to touch it.

She nods and pulls my hand to her chest.

The web is hot against my palm, teeming with the warmth of life and love. When I close my eyes, I catch racing images of Revalia and my life together—our experiences as training humans, our experiences as adversaries, our experiences from before our dawn, things even I haven't remembered for the longest time come flooding into me. A millennia of knowing. A millennia of friendship, kinship, and guardianship. We always were and always had been, and the threads sing songs of our very astral genes. But these memories should be mine, and mine alone.

She closes her eyes, sighs deeply, and smiles. I almost don't have the heart to tell her that she's failed.

Again.

For the last time.

I press firmly on her chest, my claws digging into the upper layer of her astral flesh. Her eyes open wide with a wild look of disbelief. "What are you..." she tries to say, but it's too late. I've already sunk a claw into her and pierced beneath the surface. Viciously, I dig in and root around for a viable piece of her string. She gasps for air at my assault, but I place a finger on her lips and tell her to "hush." My magic seals her lips together so that she can't protest, can't scream out, can't try to persuade me with her angelic words.

Soon, I am able to get one of the thin spindly pieces of string wrapped around my fingertip, and I withdraw my claw from her chest pulling it out slowly. She squeals as the web unravels from her chest like seams untangling from a piece of clothing. I pull and pull at the highway of fibers—the colors and lights die the second they leave her body. And the more I pull, the wider she becomes—a gaping hole forms at the center of her chest and pulls back her astral pieces in a circular undoing. Bursts of her light shock me and punch me in the face. She screams, begging me to stop pulling her apart. But I continue to unravel Revalia as a memory dawns on me...

*When I was a child, a human child*, I had a rag doll made from cheap fabric. I had named her Valeria—maybe something in my astral gene was trying to recreate my angel friend—and I had kept that doll close to me always, for years upon years. Until one day, Valeria started to fray and come undone at her seams. Curious as I was, curious as any seven-year-old child would be, I pulled at the threadbare edges until Valeria disappeared in front of my eyes. Like magic. Like she didn't exist. Like she never existed, because I know she didn't, not really. I know me being a human child wasn't real, it didn't happen. But it did, because somebody else out there remembers that it did, so it must have...

And in my scattered memories and questioning reality, I continue to pull out the very fabric that kept Revalia together—the thoughts and memories of her beloved Aestra. But Aestra is gone, and now Revalia is too. I pull her out until there is nothing left but a pile of string draped over a dead angel's body.

I cannot marvel at my work for too long because I am grabbed from behind with some kind of magic tether. It paralyzes me, and I drop my sword to my side. Drakonas and Uriah speak swiftly to one another, and I am unable to move my head to try to read their lips. I can make out the words, "Go," and "Now," but everything around me gets hazy. I am angry that I let my guard down for that long, that I let myself get swept away in my murderous rage. The haze consumes me, and everything goes black.

CHAPTER THIRTEEN

## THE REDEEMER

"Is she okay?"

"Does it hurt to be up there like that?"

"Will she ever be able to come down?"

"Does she know what she's done?"

"Are you sure she's the one you've told us about?"

"She sure doesn't look anything like I imagined her to be!"

Voices drift up to my ears on the cusp of a warm breeze, and slowly my eyes begin to flutter open. The bright light from the sun on the horizon makes it hard for me to adjust my vision to my surroundings, but from what I can see, there is nothing but orange and beige and clay colored sand for miles around me.

*Miles below me.*

Somehow, I am suspended in air. I crane my head downward and see the source of the chattering voices. A group of little children are gathered at my feet, pointing up at me, staring, gawking, *oohing* and *aaaahh-ing*. They have bright light faces that mask the true vision of their appearance and they wear white robes with scarlet ropes tied at their waists. I'm still piecing everything together when one of them points and says, "Her blood is red!"

I look to my right and then down at my naked body, and it all comes together. I am high off the ground, my arms spread at my sides and thick iron nails have been driven through my wrists to hold me in place to a cross of wood at my back. A puncture wound runs deep along the line of my ribcage, and the lower part of my body is drenched in blood. I have been crucified, but not in just any way. I have been crucified in the manner of the Redeemer, sealed, and trapped and held in place in this great expanse of a desert. When the realization hits me, I feel the pain for the first time and gasp for air.

"She's awake! She's awake!" one of the children shouts and they all clamor closer to me to get a look. Tiny hands brush up against my open toes. One of them tugs at the rope that binds my feet to the wood and I cry out from the sting of the twine rubbing against my scraped flesh.

"Easy, children. Easy," a gentle voice says from the crowd of kids.

He glides among them leaving a trail of glittery white light with each stride. Bushy brown hair frames his beard-covered face so that all I can see is the tip of his nose and his calming dark brown eyes. That's all I need to see, though. The children gravitate to him when he appears like flies swarming to honey. When he outstretches his arms, they pile in close to him and engulf themselves within his peaceful aura. The beard on his face moves upward and I know he is smiling, enjoying their devotion and love. It is no secret the Great Teacher had a special bond with children, for it is said that only children can love with a pure and untainted heart, and only the Son of God had that child-like innocence even after he was crucified, died, and was buried. It is also no secret that he is a great storyteller, and I put up my guard, knowing I will have to watch his words carefully.

"Now run along, my little lambs," he says to them.

"Oh, please, Lord, let us stay a little while longer with you!" one of them pleads.

He bends down on his knees, reaching them at eye level, and they stare at him intently, lovingly. "No, no," he commands in a firm, yet tender voice. "We will meet again later. I promise." They smile at him, and they scatter into the desert. Some hold hands and gently glide over the hot sand, some fly up high into the sky, casting shadows on the dune pits below them. Their tinkling voices echo along the horizon, singing songs of worship and praise, and he watches them adoringly as they melt away in the distance.

When they are all out of earshot and sight, the Redeemer turns his head upward to look at me. "Aestrangel," he says softly. "Hello, sister."

I hang my head low to meet his gaze, and even though there is some space between us, I catch a glimpse of my reflection in his deep brown eyes. In my raw nakedness, my eyes reflect with a preternatural purple glow. *So that's where Revalia is*, I muse to myself as the Redeemer crosses his arms in front of him. Blood from my swollen lip pools in my mouth, and I spit it onto the sand below me ... right at his feet. He doesn't move though. The sight of it disturbs him not. He's seen worse, been through worse.

"Where am I? Where is this place?" I ask.

"This is The Second Heaven. Father gave me dominion here."

"Who are they?" I say, motioning my head in the direction which the children departed.

"They are the discarded ones. Souls of the children who were thrown away before they even had a chance. I watch over them now. Let the children come to me. Let the children come. Never hinder them, never stop them," he says in a musical voice.

The only time I have ever been in the son's presence was on the day he ascended to Ilarium, and I have never traversed to this sacred place, but something about it seems familiar. Something resonates inside of me as I search my mind and memory for more secrets and lies to uncloud my vision. Then, suddenly, my heart drops a little. I remember the stories of The Second Heaven and what it means for the souls who pass through there. "You choose the Ishim, don't you? But what about the three judges in the Hall of Mirrors?" I say.

He nods. "It is more than determining the souls who are worthy for Ishim." He extends his arm to the horizon behind him. "Before a human soul can get to the Hall, they must trek the wide open to get there. The road to redemption leads through deserts."

I roll my head, and my eyes look all about my wooden cross. "This? Is this a way to coerce some sort of redemption from me? Or is this the punishment that Michael spoke of before our battle?"

"That's up to you to decide, Aestrangel. If you are to repent, you must die on the cross. Repent therefore, and turn again, that your sins may be blotted out. Because truly, unless one is born again, he cannot see the true kingdom of God."

I laugh as a searing pain shrieks through my arms. "You all keep talking about redemption as if it's something I want."

"But you do. You don't realize it yet. I probably know you better than anyone else, Aestrangel. You and I were created in very similar ways, with very similar thoughts and dreams and desires. We are of the same ilk."

"Don't presume that we are anything alike, Yeshua!" I growl and more blood sprays from behind my teeth covering the Redeemer's face in a fine, red mist.

"Fair enough," he relents and places his hands on my feet. "You've certainly amassed great power over the course of your existence. Your star shines so bright that it practically blots out the hottest sun in the entire cosmos. A flash so blinding that you leave behind a gaping darkness in your wake. I know the plans the Lord has for you. They are plans for good and not for disaster, to give you a future and a hope. If you give him Camael, what's left of Camael, you will be able to change the course of everything."

Apophis coils inside me, doubling my upper torso over with a wrenching soreness. I try to calm it down, but I don't think it can hear me. The iron nails in my wrists and the binding at my feet have locked me in place, and try as I may, I can't dig deep enough inside to access my power from within. The Great Teacher has protected himself well from me, and he has chosen his words carefully. Yes, he speaks of Camael. And if he wants to go head-to-head and quote holy scripture, well, I can do that all day long too. But he spoke of the great power I have amassed, and Apophis stirred. There's more than Camael that they want from me.

Sweat begins to form on my brow as the sun climbs higher in the sky. It beats down on me, securing me in place with its stinging rays. A thirst forms in my throat, and my powerless body struggles for the upper hand, but the only weapon I have now is my venomous words. "So, this is my punishment?" I growl dryly. "You've re-created your final days as a human for me? Is this what it was like for you? Were your powers stripped of you too? Weren't you left begging for the creator to help you? You were just as helpless and powerless up there on your cross, *Brother*. Father left you there, unable to free yourself, and unwilling to help you." I muster up what energy I can from the depths of my stomach and use the voice of the Redeemer to echo his own words back at him, "Abba! Why have you forsaken me?" I groan in his voice. He shifts uncomfortably and a flash of terror streaks across his face, but he remains steadfast, unmoved.

I laugh and more blood spills from my mouth. It pools below me in the sand sitting in a dark red lake above the beige dusty earth.

"Tricks," he says matter-of-factly. "You seem to have mastered a few."

"More than you know. Behold! I am doing a new thing—it will spring forth, and all will perceive it. It will make its way through the wilderness and fashion rivers in the desert," I say, spouting scripture back at him with my own twist on the holy words.

He pauses, bends down, and pulls from his robes a pitcher of water. "So, Aestrangel, if you are so strong, if you have mastered more than mere illusions and lies, why don't you bring yourself down from that cross and drink with me from this holy cup, Sister."

He's testing me. Tempting me. Apophis turns its snake body inside out and expands into tentacles up and down the length of my body. Suddenly, one of the iron nails pushes forward from the cross, but I stop it from releasing me.

"Ahh," he sighs, "newborn babies crave pure spiritual milk, and from that you shall grow in your salvation. You have tasted your own. You know that the Lord is good. Why deny the glory of Hosanna the Highest?"

"To come down from here and drink with you would be an admission of guilt. I am guilty of nothing."

"But Father nurtured us with his own divinity. Don't you want the same for..."

"You are smarter than that, Yeshua. A part of me is still angel divine. That may have worked on some lesser daimon, but I am well versed in the Law of Abode. To accept food or drink from my captor would be me accepting my place here in your realm. And we both know I'm not up for Ishim like the other souls who pass through your gates. Besides, one does not live by drink alone," I spit his own words back at him again.

He nods at me knowingly, lingering in his own memory. He had once been tempted like this in a similar desert. "I know, Aestrangel. All of this is confusing and strange. It is for all of us. Your story is unprecedented and has shaken the fabric of our entire existence."

"As was yours," I acknowledge.

"Why can't you open your angel heart to the love of our Father? Or even your human heart?" he persists. "Honor your Father, so that you may live long in the land the Lord your God gives to you."

I huff through a wave of pain. "The land he gives me? And what's your definition of 'living?'"

He puts out his hands palms up. "You know the answer to that." He waves his arm behind him, and different scenes appear in the sky—Ilarium, The Observatory, the cosmos, all the realms of divinity. "All these things He will give you if you fall and repent. If you dedicate yourself to a penitent life and dedicate yourself to the Lord your God, you will be forgiven and at peace. The Lord will fight for you; you need only to be still."

*Forgiven? At peace?* I've seen first-hand how the creator forgives. I've witnessed how he doles out his version of peace, and that's not something I care to subscribe to.

The Redeemer puts down his pitcher of holy water at the base of the cross. "Unlike your demonic consorts, if you threw yourself from the cross right now, a holy host of angels would swoop down and break your fall. They would save you, Aestrangel, because you are worth saving. They would save you because our Father still believes there is good in you. There is a spark, an energy that is special to Him."

*Apophis.* He speaks of Apophis. The creator cast me out when I rejected him. He abandoned me when I needed him most. And now? Now I am a spark that is special. After I murdered one of his most valuable allies? No. It's not me, or even Camael for that matter, but what's brewing inside me. My new spark. My self-created energy. The creator wants that for himself. Wants to pick me apart and inspect every inch of my essence. Save the power and wield it against Lucifer. Against me.

I narrow my eyes. "Why would I believe that, Yeshua? Don't you know what he did to me? Do you forget what he did to *you*?"

"And do you forget what you did to Him? To all of us?"

"I forget nothing."

"So, end this now, Aestrangel. You can end all of this, and we can all start anew. Our Father, who art in Heaven, hallowed is His name. He forgives you. He will show you mercy if you have true sorrow in your heart." He reaches his hand for me to come down from the cross.

The Messiah is kind and warm just like a child. A glowing halo forms about his head, and he smiles so gently, so sincerely, that his love for the Father shines through in his demeanor most pure.

But I remain in my agonizing position as the sun beats down harder on my gray skin. I linger there somewhere between my bulletproof obstinacy and wavering thoughts of redemption. The Great Teacher regales me with tales of his walk on Earth, and I am so racked with my own agony, I feel as if I actually stood beside him on his adventures. I helped him destroy the gambling tables in the temple when we were kids, I held his hand as we walked across the water together, I spoke the words to change that water into wine at the wedding feast at Cana, and I raised my hand to command Lazarus to walk again. All these stories are a weapon to try to lull me into submission.

And unexpectedly, just as the son is about the begin the story of his last journey into Jerusalem, the ground beneath me rumbles and splits open—the sand falls into a great chasm and sputtering up from the dank hole is burning hot magma, hellfire from the darkest pits of Gehenna. The Redeemer falls backward at the base of my cross. His back cracks against the wood with a thud. Slowly, a shape manifests from the crevasse—a massive monolith of black stone riddled with fissures of oozing lava. The shape rises high above the horizon, masking the sun, creating an instantaneous darkness in the Redeemer's domain. I don't need to see the Ibex horns to know that it's Lucifer. The cavalry has come.

But I am weak—weary from the War, weary from the cross, weary from the persistence of the sun and the son.

"Sataniel," the Redeemer says in a confused voice.

Lucifer pays him no mind and saunters over to me on the cross. With his gargantuan fingers, he plucks me from the wood like a child plucking petals from a flower. The iron nails slide through my astral skin and bone as two fonts of blood burst open and douse the Great Teacher below. He is bathed in it, stained with my corruption.

"Sacrifices should be consummated in blood," Lucifer snarls in the ancient tongue. He raises his hand high in the air, and for a split second, I think he is going to end the life of the Redeemer.

Yeshua looks at me, "Daughter," he gurgles through a mouthful of my blood, "behold your Father. Father, behold your daughter."

Lucifer nods, and relaxes his arm, sparing the Redeemer's life. He then places me in the palm of his hand and closes his fingers over me in a protective way.

"It is finished," Yeshua mutters as I wrap my arms around Lucifer's claw. He hops on his cloven hooves back into the void in the ground, and we descend.

# CHAPTER FOURTEEN

# THE REASON

*We've won.*

According to Lucifer, the Order of the Daimones was victorious over the Order of the Angelos. The holy host was the first to retreat, thus giving the win to our side. After the defeat of Michael, Lucifer got him to confess my location and the plan they had for me. Lucifer said it took all his strength and power to pierce through the heart of The Second Heaven, and that I had been there for quite some time. It didn't feel that way, though, but I guess time moves differently in that realm because it felt as if I was there for just a moment. Lucifer also said it had been a long time since he had to use his monolith form, and that I should be grateful for his efforts to retrieve me from that place.

*I am grateful.* I remember my darkest days in Asphodel when I first fell from Ilarium, no one came to help me. I had begged and pleaded and called out across the cosmos, but the angelic troops were nowhere to be seen or heard. In my greatest time of need, who was there but the Prince of Darkness himself. My savior. My redeemer. A true father coming to the rescue of his child.

"We may have won the battle, Aestrangel, but we still have much more work to do," Lucifer says as we return to Gehenna. His titanic body slowly transforms to the figure I am most familiar with—the dark Hades shape that exudes dashing wickedness. As he whittles down in size, he effortlessly throws me over his shoulder like a frayed ragdoll, battered and bruised. Thank someone my thread isn't showing from the seams, lest I end up frazzled and tattered like Valeria or end up a pile of useless string like Revalia.

"B... But Yeshua said," I mumble. It's hard to get out my words. My time with the Redeemer has markedly taken its toll.

"Yes, dear, he said it was finished. He seems to like saying that doesn't he?" Lucifer smirks. "But he meant that chapter, that moment in time. Their quest to contain you is finished because you cannot be contained. I told them that though. They should have listened. It would have saved them a lot of trouble and dead brethren."

"Why didn't you kill him?" I ask. "Why didn't you destroy the son?"

"I can't. It's not allowed. It's part of my deal with god. Just like he can't kill you."

I struggle to understand. "B... But Yeshua said," I find myself repeating, "Yeshua said that I would have to die on the cross in order to repent and be forgiven."

"Of your own will, Aestrangel. They could not kill you outright, but had you agreed to their terms, it would have been like giving them permission."

"B... B... But..." My words fail me.

"Hush, child," he says. "You need to rest. You need to build your strength back up." He strokes my naked back with his sharp fingernails and stops at my steel wing branches. "These are just *dying* to fully bloom!" My body goes limp, and I am silent the rest of the way back to the throne room.

The halls of Gehenna are eerily quiet as Daimones, both new and old, sit in their spaces, lick their wounds, and reflect upon the battle Lucifer claims they have won. Ask an angel, and I bet their answer would be quite similar. They were able to get the upper-hand, capture the strange angel, and remand me into the custody of the Redeemer. I could see how they would call that a victory for their side. A pensive silence sweeps through the caverns, and I can't help but think the same silence overtakes Ilarium as well. The battle wasn't a true victory for either of us. No one won. Not really. Both sides have suffered great losses, and both sides are still reeling from their battle scars. To say one was dominant over the other is left to a matter of perception because a case could be made for the glory of either one. Lucifer has to boast of their victory because if they believe they lost, he will have a bigger problem on his hands.

When we reach the throne room, Lucifer sets me on the stone ground and wraps his arm around my waist to hold me up. I look to my seat next to his and see that someone has retrieved my armor from the Astral Plane. My helmet sits on the chair with my gallant sword by its side. My coat of mail hangs from the back. I make a motion to sit in my place, but he quickly ushers me to the corner where Lilith rests. "Woman!" he calls to her. "Leave your place. Aestrangel needs to lie down!"

Lilith coils her neck to the side, narrows her eyes at me in disgust, and sighs loudly.

"Now!" he commands in a booming voice.

Baby bones crunch underneath her as she slowly slithers down from her perch, and a venomous slime trails behind her. Lucifer sweeps me up into his arms and carries me over the bed so that my bare toes do not step in her toxic wake. Each movement is slow and deliberate, for I know her hatred and jealousy for me is deep and wide. I am too weak to give it much thought, but if I can displace her from her bed, does she think I can displace her from her position in Gehenna? She slithers down the hallway of the room and into the darkness of the cave, her tail rattling wildly the farther away she gets to let us know she is unhappy with this situation.

Lucifer lays me on the bed and calls for Malek and Alukah to assist him. "Now, now," he whispers to me. "Pay no attention to Lilith. She's gotten bitter in her older years. I will soothe her jealous heart later. You worry about getting strong again."

The bed is soft, outfitted in black velvet blankets that swallow me in their depths. I extend my legs out as Lucifer gathers my black hair at the top of my head and drapes it over the edge of the bed. I am sprawled out and exposed, and as I settle my breathing to a steady flow of inhales and exhales, the stinging and throbbing of my wounds reverberates throughout my body.

Lucifer looks me up and down, drinking in the vision of my nakedness, marveling at every inch of my body. "Look at you!" he sighs in delight. "Even in your blood-stained state, even in your weakest moment, you are still a dream of loveliness." He strokes my cheek with the backs of his fingers and kisses me on the forehead. As he draws his face away from mine, I reach for the back of his icy neck and hold him in place, staring into the depths of his jet-black eyes.

"You saved me," I say breathlessly. "You saved me from myself. There are no words in any tongue that can explain and express my eternal gratitude."

He smiles, flashing me the full extent of his devilish charms. I filled his demon heart—touched him deep in his core. That look I will never forget. That look I will hold in my memory for the rest of my days, for it was the purest and truest response I have ever seen from Lucifer.

And it will stay with me because I will use it to my advantage someday.

See, unlike him—unlike any of them, really—I speak the truth and come with no presuppositions. I am grateful. I am thankful. I am happy that I am safe here under him. I'm even more thankful that Apophis is safe and that Malek is safe and that the war feels like it's coming to some strange resolution. I have seen through time and space and dimensions and planes, and I have seen the end—felt the end, felt *through* the end and *into* the end and *beyond* the end. And there, I have seen only me and a world of my design.

Lucifer runs his fingers down the length of my body sending tsunamis of chills against my astral skin. He caresses every crease of the gray flesh. He presses on my open wounds and squishes the exposed tissue. He grips the crevice between my legs, inserts his fingers, and strokes my insides as if he's claiming me. Alukah glides over to the bed and nuzzles her head on Lucifer's shoulder. "Alukah will clean you up. Lie still and let her heal you," he says. His fingers linger inside me a little longer until he finally steps away.

Alukah pulls her hood down, and her strange face jars me. It twists and turns from a smile to a frown to a growl to a laugh to a smirk to a scowl, and the only defining point of her face is her teeth. She climbs on top of me and latches on to my arm, bobbing her head up and down on the place where the iron nail impaled me to the cross. Her vampire teeth grip the ragged hole on my wrist, and she laps at my astral blood. With each lick of her tongue, the flesh begins to close up on itself. Quickly, she moves to my other arm and mends that wound as well. With her hands placed firmly on my breasts, she inches down further to the gash on my ribcage and works the same healing magic there, only this time she works slowly, diligently. She savors me and delights in the flavor of my essence. Her moans of enjoyment echo in the throne room each time her tongue dances inside the laceration. When she has finally sealed me up and has had her fill of my aura, her head snaps up with a glowing clown smile, and she climbs down from the bed to take her leave.

Already, I am feeling better.

I feel even better when Malek comes to me.

He saunters into the room and climbs into the bed with me. He covers my face and neck with hundreds of sweet and soft kisses and pulls the edge of the velvet blanket up and over my naked body to cover me and make me feel comforted. Like he's claiming me. "What's the story, Morning Glory?" he says playfully with raised eyebrows.

The storm swirls in his gray eyes, and when I catch his stare, it calms to a summer rain shower with a violet rainbow glistening on the horizon. I know he is reflecting the new color of my eyes, and my face gets hot with a pink blush. "You brought my armor back," I say matter-of-factly.

"But, of course," he smiles and looks over to the throne.

"How did you..."

"I always know," he interrupts. "I always know where and how to find you. From the very beginning. It's how I found you on Earth and in Asphodel every time..."

"But..." my voice trails.

He lowers his brow with a "Are you serious?" look, and I think of Malek and his power. His great and boundless power. And I think of how I really never gave any thought to it before this moment. Malek's power. He is the storm, yet he is the beacon in the storm. And he is the shape-shifter in the night. And he is the creator of nightmares and the seer of things in this world and beyond. He is the artificer of illusion and glamouring. I wonder if the arch-angel Michael really did tell Lucifer of my whereabouts. Maybe it was Malek all along who found me through space and time—he has before. And he *will* again.

"How are you?" he asks, breaking me from my thoughts.

"Okay, I guess," I respond, shifting in the bed to give him more room next to me.

He rubs his hand across the velvet covers, petting me, calming me. "Good. It's not over, you know."

I nod.

"You know you've been away for some time, don't you?"

I nod again. "Yes, I'm aware."

"Their plan has changed."

I pause, plugging every possible outcome into my mind until I come to a likely possibility. "They don't want me anymore," I say boldly. "They've given up on me, haven't they?"

"In a way, yes," he says. "The rumbling through the cosmos is that you are too fragile to contain. They still want what is left of Camael, and they know there is something about you, something *else* inside you that..."

"Apophis," I whisper unintelligibly.

He nods. "You are much too important to them now. They do not want to risk anything happening to you until they can extract what they want to extract. They want to take Lucifer head on, and I think they are hoping that they will be able to get to you through him."

My arms wrap protectively around my stomach, the way a pregnant woman would shield their child nesting in the womb.

"And the place where you were... did you see him?" Malek continues. "Did you meet with The Great Teacher?"

"Oh, yes," I say bitterly.

"So, you know? I'm sure he told you, then. Regardless of whether or not the Angelos extract Camael from you, regardless of whether or not they can investigate and study your astral gene, regardless of whether or not they think they can contain you or me, or Lucifer or our entire Order, this War between our kind and theirs is never going to end. Not the way they think they can end it. It will rage on for all of eternity, and we will be forced to fight until the end of time because what our father wants... what they will never give him."

I sit up in the bed, clutching the velvet blanket to my chest. "What do you mean?" I practically shout with confusion. "Yeshua never said anything like that! What are you talking about? He said it was finished."

"You really don't know?" he says, sitting up next to me.

"No, Malek!" I yell, shaking my head. "I don't know! I mean, I have my theories, but I'm not one hundred percent sure."

He inhales deeply, and on the exhale, a puff of preternatural smoke escapes his lips. "The only thing that will end this conflict is an apology, Aestrangel. A simple apology from the creator—an apology for creating the humans, an apology for the Punishment of Lilith, an apology for abandoning Lucifer and the other fallen angels. See, everyone apologizes *to* god. Humans beg for his forgiveness when they sin. For eons, he's heard scores upon scores of apologies, even from mankind's most deviant delinquents, and he's forgiven even the vilest among them. But never has he uttered an apology for what he has done. Never has he asked for anyone's forgiveness because he's always been better and above everyone else. But that does not mean he hasn't transgressed. As a matter of fact, time and time again, we've seen he's sometimes the worst offender of us all."

It's hard to wrap my mind around this nugget of information. "I thought it was all about power and control and domination and supremacy! And you're telling me all this time, all this chaos and plotting and planning and destruction and war, and all Lucifer wants is for the creator to say he's sorry?"

Malek runs his fingers through my hair and brings the end strands up to his nose to inhale my scent. He picks up on my confusion and annoyance and wants to breathe in the smell of it all. It smells like oranges fresh off the branch. It's a strong aroma that tantalizes him. "Yes, Aestrangel, that's exactly what I'm saying."

-PART III-
# THE RISEN

*"Jealousy. What do you know of jealousy? Do you know what it feels like? Because, Aestra, the one who knew what jealousy felt like was the first to fall. He was most loved by the Creator. He was called the Morning Star. When he fell, it was like lightning piercing the center of the Earth for the first time. You are Aestra. My Star. And you are most loved by me. Do you understand?"*

—CAMAEL

## CHAPTER FIFTEEN

# THE REVEAL

*An apology?*

All of this—all the manufactured pain and suffering was all predicated on Lucifer needing someone to say "Sorry?" The concept boggles my weary mind, sends me into a mental tailspin, and makes my heart rate jump to heights I've never felt pounding in my chest. It also doesn't help that Apophis twists inside me with its growth spurt. It grinds and burns me from within as all the souls and spirits I have amassed congeal together like some homunculus experiment. I understand the Angelos want the essence of Camael back in Ilarium, but I've compiled such an immense body of work, I'm not even sure pure Camael is still there. Has he too been infected with my demonic brethren?

"I'm tired," I say to Malek as I turn over onto my side.

He gets up from the bed. "Of course. If you need me, call me. If you want me, call louder."

I smile; he can't see it, but it's wide and bright and sends glitter lights about the room. He puts his hand on the back of my neck and presses gently before leaving the throne room. I know he smiled back. I envision his perfect white teeth illuminating against my smile shine.

*We do make a perfect pair, don't we?* My mind's voice screams as he flies through Gehenna.

"We always did," I hear him in my head. "It was you that needed a little convincing."

"Absolutely not!" I scoff back. "You rejected me not so long ago, if I recall correctly!"

"You must not be that tired if you're yelling at me!" he jokes.

"I know, I know," I relent. "Going now."

"Rest, Morning Glory," he says to me, and I feel him tune his mind off to me. I open my mouth to say goodbye but stop myself. The darkness, the *blankness*, in the space between us is like a roadblock, and I know anything I say won't be heard; as soon as Malek is gone from my mind, I drift right back to where I left off.

*Camael. Are you still there? Is some fragment of your former self still residing in my core?*

I close my eyes and let my mind's eye take over. I envision myself somersaulting into the depths of my essence and traversing the deep and complicated highways that make me *me*. I silence the sound of the flittering harpy wings in the cavern, and put myself at ease, at rest, and I listen for the sounds of each individual life crying, screaming, and singing inside.

Alukah said I couldn't create, but she was wrong. I did create. I did design. But my design was much different than what everyone wanted. The deeper I view inside myself, the more I come to see that Apophis is a vessel, a holding cell, a prison for all the beings I ingested. But it, too, is transforming. The beings are coming together in a way I never imagined possible, and making Apophis, *Apophis*—a new being altogether. And Apophis is strong, for it is the melding of demonic and angelic matter, but it is slowly but surely taking on a life of its own, developing its own power and...

*Free will.*

And that's the scariest aspect of this creature I harbor. I'm not sure how long I can keep it inside, for I fear that *it* will begin to devour me.

"Camael," I whisper. "Where are you?"

I hold my breath and scan the silence. I reach my astral wings and flash their lights like a signal fire calling to some far away wanderer. In the void of my being, in the depths of my core, something flickers back. Like a smile. Like a wink of an eye. Its warmth seeps throughout my insides and goosebumps rise to my astral skin, and I know it's him shining in my darkness. There's a slight sliver of him left like the thin, upturned smile of the waning moon. "Aestra, my star, where are *you*?" he whispers to me, and I can't help but smile back. He's been there all this time— whispering to me, trying to guide me. My own inner voice drowned him out, and I was barely aware of his presence, then the voices of the others drowned him out even more, making him the least audible to my essence.

"I've been here the whole time, Camael," I say.

"You were always the brightest," he says in a low voice. "But you're consumed by the darkness now."

"I am the Darkness. I consume it. It doesn't consume me."

"But you can shine still. It isn't too late."

Before I can continue communicating with him, Apophis growls, and the giant cloud of its hand covers the sliver of Camael and blocks him out.

I open my eyes, coming back to the throne room, coming back to the reality of Lilith's baby-bone bed, pushing the thoughts of Camael away. I begin to think about what Malek said to me before he left.

*Apology.*

It seems so simple. It seems so trivial. It seems so *stupid.*

I was taught to be wary of Lucifer from the dawn of my creation. I was taught that he was the most vile and evil Prince of Lies. In his most wretched form, as Sataniel, I was taught that he was the Great Manipulator, the Supreme Destroyer, He Who Holds the Lightning Rod. He who tempted Eve and brought sin into the world. He who made mountains quake and tempted Yeshua in the desert. He who laid to waste the humans through the mere power of suggestion. All these monikers to exemplify his wickedness. All these names to convey the most dreadful visions in the minds and hearts of the Angelos and the humans on Earth. It was said that Lucifer hated the humans. Was jealous of them. Fell from on high because of his anger at the creator and envy of his most divine creation. But all this time, those were lies.

Yes, Lucifer was jealous. His creator had turned his attention to his new plaything and all but ignored his holy host.

Yes, Lucifer was livid. When he fell in love with Lilith, he was still an obedient servant in the creator's court, but his love was brutalized behind his back. So, yes. There is real justification behind Lucifer's anger. God made him suffer. He made Lilith suffer.

But the end result doesn't seem to fit. Over the course of time, Lucifer burned cities to the ground, drove humans to madness, tortured and maimed and flexed his demonic muscle in every depraved way known to man and beyond. All for an apology? From God?

I can't rectify it in my mind. I can't wrap my head around the concept.

*If all Lucifer wanted was an apology, why didn't the creator give it to him?*

Because wouldn't that have solved a lot of these issues in the first place?

I recall the conversation between Lucifer and the Archangel Michael right before we went to battle. Lucifer had said, "You know what I want." To which Michael responded, "And you know that will never happen." I'm quite certain they were talking about the apology.

My stomach flip-flops over the thought of it, sickened by the simplicity and stupidity of it all. Lucifer's years of torment and torture were just a little child trying to get his daddy's attention! "Daddy, Daddy! Look at me! You hurt my feelings! Make things right!"

Disgraceful!

Disgusting!

Angels and humans alike actually fear this sham of a Dark Ruler! He is nothing but a sniveling child! And angels and humans alike actually worship the creator, the ineffectual puppet master!

Lucifer doesn't want to take control. He doesn't want to rule the cosmos. He wants his father to say "Sorry" for wronging him. Whatever that means! Because, what if one day god decides enough is enough? What if god gives in and says, "Ya know what? I do apologize for all this." Where does that leave the Morning Star? Does he want to

continue his reign as the Supreme Leader of Evil, or does he go back to Ilarium to be reunited with the Lord? So many questions. So many possibilities. So many variables that leave the future of Gehenna in a state of uncertainty. I don't like states of uncertainty. I don't like variables. If I ruled this realm, I *would* punch a hole in the cosmos so deep the angels and the humans would truly have something to fear. They would have a real reason to worship and beg and forgive and rejoice—not some False Hades pretending to be the epitome of true malevolence. I would show them the meaning of true malevolence. I would show them what it truly means to tremble in the face of the Dark.

*And I will.*

I close my eyes again and listen to the wails and lamentations of the chorus inside me. It swells to a jangling din like sleigh bells gone wild on their tethers. The song makes everything seem so clear and in focus, and I understand the intentions of the creator with a clarity I had never felt before. Like the thin veil of newborn naïveté has just been raised from my eyes.

*This was always the plan.*

The creator was bored with the Angelos. He was bored with their songs and admiration, and wanted something else to fill whatever void was inside Him. When god created the humans, he anticipated something like this would happen. He anticipated the jealousy, the anger, the Fall of the Angelos. Lucifer fell because of Lilith, the first woman. That *had* to happen, because with this new creation of humankind, there needed to be a balance of good and evil. Before the dawn of man, it was all one-sided. It was all peace and love, and joy and supreme happiness. The angels worshipped god with unconditional love and obedience. They praised him with their eternal devotion, but when the lord expanded his lot, he knew it couldn't just be one way, one side. He knew that for the people to be truly in service to him, there needed to be a degree of conflict. Earth was not Ilarium, and with the humans so far removed from the heavenly realm, it would be harder for them to bask in his hallowed glory, so the creator needed an ounce of conflict. He *needed* Lucifer to fall. Because without conflict, there's no story—no history to be told or remembered, and with no one to remember the story, god, essentially, wouldn't exist. There would not be a driving force to guide the humans' concept of *faith.*

*God was looking to give meaning to his own existence by manipulating evil into the world. And with it, he sacrificed the integrity of all his creations.*

So where do I fit in to all of this? What is my designed role from the spark of my creation? What do I ultimately want, and do I really want it, or is it another pre-determined eye on a spoke of Uriah's Wheel? Why did the creator form me from the purest star-matter only to watch me as angel and as human and as demon—transformed into the shape of each one of his supreme creations? Was that for his amusement? Experimentation? Evolutionary trials? Why did he give me agency over myself when so many others are bound to their pre-set agendas? So he could watch me rise and fall and rise and fall again?

*Because I will eventually rise again.*

And I'm not sure he will step back and marvel at his creation this time around. For if he truly had any inclination of what he has done, he might be more inclined to dole out some of those apologies more willingly. An apology for making me suffer, an apology for making Lucifer suffer, and Lilith suffer, and the humans suffer, and his own son suffer. But he's too proud, resting way high up there on his laurels to even consider his own mistakes. He is lord! He has made no mistakes! I laugh at the ridiculousness of it. I cry because, at one time, I was stupid enough to believe it.

Apophis is the one wild card in all of this because that is the one creation that didn't come directly from the creator himself, and I'm not quite sure how far the Angelos are willing to go to get their astral paws on it. This might warrant an apology from the creator, after all. I know they are desperate—itching to get a hold of me and rip me apart to see what's inside. It's not just Camael they want. In fact, they may have given up hope on him. They know something lurks and brews in my core, and they want to see. No. He wants to see. He *needs* to see. He needs to see the one, true thing that is not of his making, not of his design. It must be driving him crazy with curiosity—he who is the Alpha and Omega, Artificer of the Cosmos and all that is beautiful and ugly within being faced with the knowledge that there is an intruder in his midst—a powerful force he did not commission or devise. To think that it drives him mad is delicious!

And now I know.

I know what it will take to set me on my path. To be the True Dark Star in the inky black night, I will need to somehow get rid of the Morning Star. Because that's what I was designed to do, isn't it? For only a creature of angel and human and demonic ilk could truly understand the meaning of balance and rule accordingly. Not a sniveling child begging for his father to say sorry. Not some romanticized fallen angel trying to avenge the honor of his love. For who better to bring balance to the cosmos than the strange angel? For who better to rule with sheer force and malice and no other intentions but those than the strange angel? I want to be worshipped at the altar of the moon, and the stars, and the morning glories. I want them all to quiver at the sound of my name—just because. Because I can.

My steel wings twitch against my back, and the metal quills sprout up sharp blades in place of feathers. The new feathers tear holes in the velvet blanket as they stretch and grow. Something like a chuckle rumbles me inside. Apophis is pleased with my newest upgrade.

As am I.

## CHAPTER SIXTEEN

# THE BIRTHING

I'm enjoying my time of convalescence in the throne room but know it won't last long. It has been nearly seven days of rest and relaxation, and I've grown stronger with each passing hour. Demons of Lucifer's bidding attended to me and brought me anything my heart desired. He had instructed them to do as I commanded and to fulfill my every whim. I was careful not to overdo it, not to cross certain lines and make outlandish requests, but I have to admit, it was awfully nice being taken care of like that. Amon brought me fresh-picked strawberries from the finest crops. Chemush kept the wine flowing in an onyx goblet. Ifrit made sure my sword was always at my side. Kali covered me in warm blankets. They all doted and fussed over me like a queen. Like *the* queen. I know it's two-fold: on the one hand, they were being obedient to their master, the Dark Lord, but there was something in the way they all moved around me, in the way they looked at me. They would make eye contact for a brief moment, then suddenly gaze downward. I know they are afraid of me. They know what I've done to their comrades and fear if they do something wrong or offend me in any way, they will suffer the same fate.

Little do they know there is no more room at the inn. I don't think I could hold them inside even if I tried... even if I wanted to. But I don't want to. I don't have the will or energy to allow anyone else in—to take in even the weakest of beings. My belly is full. My head is full. Sometimes their singing, and crying, and chitter-chattering on the inside is so loud that it takes all my efforts to block the sounds out. And besides, Apophis has made it very clear to me that it's taken in about as much as it can. One more soul to join the parade could very well split me apart from the inside out. And I have work to do before I would let that happen.

Malek visited every day. He calmed me and soothed me and brought me much laughter and joy. When the other demons were around, we took to speaking telepathically so they couldn't hear us. It was amusing to poke fun at them the way humans gossip behind each other's backs. It gave me raw pleasure when their demonic faces twisted in confusion at our secret laughter. They know nothing of sarcasm or humor because they have never been to the human realm, never walked in the shoes of the people, never experienced the human condition like Malek and I have. All they know is pain, and torment, and lies, and temptations, which is fine by me, but there's so much more in the cosmos to experience. It almost breaks my heart to think of how sheltered their existences really are.

So, on this seventh day, I sit up in the bed and throw my arms high in the air stretching out my limbs. I flutter my wings behind me—metal brushes against metal causing a clanking echo in the cave before I fold them back up against my back. I feel it. I feel something. Today is the day I get up from this space and...

Before I get a chance to complete my thoughts of rebellion, Lucifer enters the throne room with his entourage in tow. Alukah glides next to him in a wave of red smoke. Malek is at his left-hand side, and before I can smile brightly at him, I see a look of concern on his face that forces me to sit upright at attention. I don't like that expression. I've seen it before, and it's only meant bad things for me.

"You've rested well," Lucifer muses cheerily.

I stand up from the bed and grab my sword. "I have, thank you."

He waves a hand dismissively in front of his face. "It was important for you to gain your strength back. After everything you've been through. You are a fierce warrior, Aestrangel. I know I crowned you my General for a reason. For that, I thank you. You have not disappointed me, and I am sincerely grateful for your service."

I bow to the Dark Lord, not because I want to, but because I must. I must maintain my composure and the illusion that I serve him and him alone. When really, I want to plunge this sword deep into his gut and watch his insides spill onto the floor in front of me. I want to dance in his black ooze essence, bathe myself in it, and revel in the disgusting aura!

I serve only myself!

But still I bow, obediently, like a dutiful and gracious daughter. "Of course, Father," I say. "But without you, I would still be trapped on that cross with the son. So, for that, I am grateful for *your* service." Which is partly true. I am thankful for Sataniel's dashing rescue, but something tells me I would have eventually figured out a way to leave that desert. Lucifer said the pact he made with the creator prevents him from killing the Great Teacher, but I made no such pact, and I would have destroyed the son if it had come down to it.

Lucifer raises his eyebrows at my choice of words. "Now that you're well, I need you to do something for me."

Of course. There's always a price with Lucifer. Always an exchange. Everything he does is based on reciprocity, but always in the sense that he comes out on top or winning in the end. "What do you need me to do?" I ask, glancing over at Malek, trying to read him.

"I'm taking Alukah and Malek to see Orobas, the Oracle."

*Orobas, the Oracle.* He of horse face and bottom, with the torso of man. A shapeshifter. Demon of magicians and prophets. He cannot lie. He speaks truth bluntly and clearly. Humans summon him when they seek truth, but because there are no riddles or vague interpretations when it comes to his visions, it is said that he who summons Orobas shall face a lifetime of disappointments, for man cannot handle the blatant truth of their own existence. Orobas dwells in Sheol, a little corner of Gehenna reserved for the souls of the truth-seekers, witches and warlocks, humans who sought out the powers of the supernatural while they lived, people who dabbled in the craft of the ancients. Why Lucifer is seeking the counsel of Orobas now is a little unsettling. Malek looks uncomfortable at the mention of the Oracle's name.

"Oh," I say, my voice lilting up with a higher pitch. "Do you need me to go with you?" I ask, probing the situation.

"No," he says curtly. "This journey is for Alukah. She is ready to see. And with the threat of the Angelos ever-present, an extra layer of protection couldn't hurt."

Malek catches my attention and stares directly into my eyes. "Don't believe him," he says quietly into my mind. I hear the message, and quickly break his gaze pretending like nothing happened. I know better than to take the words of the Morning Star at face value. He's not dubbed the Prince of Lies for nothing.

"Are you sure?" I insist. "I could be of service, and…"

Lucifer smiles wide like Cheshire Cat. His face transforms with a sinister visage and shadows dance around his cheeks and the bridge of his nose. It's a haunting image that shakes me with a creepy feeling, one that even makes Apophis tingle. "Malek will be with us to assist his sister," Lucifer interrupts. "I have another plan for you, Aestrangel."

"Anything, My Lord."

"It is Lilith's time to go down to the Lake of Fire. And usually, I am there to be with her, but my meeting with Orobas can't be postponed any longer. Thankfully, this time is not a time for the birth of a living child. If it were, I would do everything in my power to be there for her. I've been there for the birth of all my children," he extends his arms and touches the shoulders of Alukah and Malek lovingly. "But still, this is an arduous ordeal for Lilith, and I don't want her to be alone. I trust you to take care of her."

I'm not keen on the idea of helping Lilith give birth. "She hates me," I blurt out and recoil after the words leave my lips.

Lucifer scoffs. "No, no, no!" he protests. "You're wrong, Aestrangel. You two haven't properly warmed up to each other. I think this is the perfect opportunity for the two of you to bond. To get closer." He smiles again, and it shoots that crawling feeling throughout my body once more.

I look at Malek, and he nods slightly letting me know he approves, that it's ok, that I should play nice and make peace with my pseudo-mother. I close my eyes and nod back. Malek is on board with me—he always has been. I know he will keep his eyes and ears open with Orobas and fill me in later. I know he will do everything in his power to protect my secret of Apophis in every way possible. In exchange, I must take care of his mother and help her through this trying time. It's the least I can do...

...*I suppose.*

—✳—✳—✴—✳—✳—

Our voyage to the Lake of Fire is a quiet one, except for all the sounds and mumblings from Lilith. As for conversation, there is none between us. Lilith slithers slowly and is near delirious in the throes of labor. Her thick tail lumbers in the dark caverns—its massive weight shifts back and forth as she moans with each contraction. The baby snakes that adorn her hair rattle their tails in unison, signifying their master's discomfort. It's like a musical parade barreling through Gehenna's corridors. Demons along our path peak out of their niches and alcoves and bow in reverence to the Dark Queen. They all know this yearly process, and all show their respect and concern for her. They all know this is a time of loss for their unholy deity.

At first, Lilith had protested Lucifer's command of me accompanying her, but after much persistence, she relented. Besides, her time was close, and I don't think she was in any shape to put up much of a fight. She hasn't spoken a word to me the entire trip over, which is fine by me. I know Lucifer wanted us to have "girl time" and to "bond," but neither of us are interested in the other, and both of us are okay with that.

The Lake of Fire is exactly that—a fiery pit surrounded by black rock crags jutting up from the surrounding ground. There is a black cliff overlooking the lake. Here, the souls of the damned, those who have renounced the creator, are sent to suffer eternal damnation. Their bodies are flung from the cliff and into the Lake, where they are either punished in a burning hell for all of eternity or transformed into a Nekudaimon, a new one. Smoke hangs heavy in the air, and a burning smell permeates the entire area. It reminds me of my time in the Black Keep when I could faintly smell the scent in the distance. This is also the place where Lilith bears her children.

Once there, she shimmies her swollen body over black rock and onto the edge of the fire. I reach for her arm to help her up, but she pulls away and hisses at me. Her hair snakes rattle wildly, and I withdraw my hand. "I've done this thousands of times," she spits. "What makes you think I need your help?"

I put my hands up defensively and bite my tongue. But she struggles. It's hard for her to hoist her bulging weight onto the rock. The green and purple iridescent scales shimmer against the fire light, and she tries so desperately to stifle her agonizing moans. It's painful to watch. It's hard to stand idly by and witness her suffering. No matter how much she hates me, no matter how much I have a certain disdain for her, it's hard to watch her go through this torment knowing what the ultimate result will be.

"Stop," I command. "Stop wiggling and use me for balance," I say lowering my shoulder in her direction."

"No," she objects, but I fan out my metal wings. I make the bladed feathers come together to form a strong handle-bar structure for her to grab onto. She narrows her eyes in a final protest, but she knows she needs me to steady herself. She concedes, exhales loudly, grips onto my wings, and hoists her heavy body up onto a smooth, flat surface among the jagged rocks. I don't expect a thank you, nor do I get one.

The underside of her tail flops to the side and the opening of her cloaca expands. The demon child will be here soon—the dead demon child that she will throw into the Lake before slithering back to her throne. Sweat forms at the crown of her head, and some of her snakes flick their forked tongues for a drink of her salty nectar. Her breathing becomes labored, and her chest heaves up and down more rhythmically, more rapidly. She's tried very hard to hush her painful groans, but she no longer can. Her grunting gets louder and louder until they crescendo to excruciating screams that mix with the sounds of the Lake's other tormented souls. Her tail rattles, and the snakes about her head jut back and forth violently in their place.

Apophis stirs. It hates this. I hate this. It's awkward and heartbreaking to watch. And then I remember. I remember a time when I tamed the snakes in the desert of the human realm. They obeyed my command and swarmed to me in submission. If I could soothe these snakes, maybe it would calm her down.

"Samael!" Lilith cries out in her delirium. "Samael, where are you? Why did you leave me here alone?"

"Lilith!" I call in a strong voice, and for a split second, all is quiet at the lake. She closes her mouth, and her snakes shift their gaze to me in unison. I crack my metal wings out at my sides and let a gentle breeze flitter in between the chrome feathers to create a hypnotizing buzz within the cave. The sound carries up and around us, filling her ears with a steady flow of white noise that lulls her. But it's not just the sound the metal blades create. The serpents' friction and rattle produce a warmth and glow that encircles me. Their tongues dart out in my direction, trying to pick up on my heat signature, trying to make their way to my calming aura. They speak to me with their eyes and send me visions of what's happening in Lilith's mind. It's fractured there, splintering between the past and the present. I urge them to keep showing me what she sees, and they send forth pictures of the beach in Nod, pictures of the Lake of Fire, pictures of cave walls decorated with sculptures of baby bones, pictures of seashells half decayed with poison salt, pictures of Samael wrapping his long arms around her waist in a loving embrace. And it's all jumbled. Muddled. A disarray of madness.

Lilith writhes on the black rock platform, and a shape begins to emerge from her widened opening. Black blood pools at the seam, and she screams out a blood curdling yelp. The snakes send me one last picture, and I know how I can comfort her.

*They send me the image of Cain.*

When Lilith and Cain had stayed together in the Land of Nod, he had been her support, her doctor of sorts, helping her give birth to the dead children into the world. I remember he told me how he had skinned the creatures and used the salt of the sea and the sand to bleach the bones in the sunlight and how he had given them to her to build her shrines. I dig deep inside myself and summon the memory of him. I scan Apophis and call forth the image of Cain, the mannerisms of Cain, the voice of Cain, the likeness of Cain. My wings flutter rapidly until I no longer hear the clanging of the chrome in the cave, until my long hair no longer feels like silk covering my breasts, until I no longer have a woman's shape. I have conjured forth a glamouring of Cain with fire red hair at my shoulders and on my face and a scar of lightning emblazoned on my muscular arm and across my back. I stand up and move over to her, unsteady on my feet at first from the alien form. I look down at my naked figure and take in full view the large man that I have become. The enormity of my general physique is dizzying, and I kneel beside Lilith is hopes that I don't double over and collapse.

"Cain?" she whispers through her deep pants.

"Yes, dear, it's me," I say. But I don't, not really. It's not just Cain's voice that I speak with, Cain is coming through, actually reaching out from the bowels of Apophis and breaking through the glamour. I shake my head back and forth from the uneasiness of the feeling. I don't like variables, and I don't like not being in control, especially over my own body, even just for a brief time.

"You've come to help me?" she moans.

"When you needed me most," he says.

"Samael asked for me to be in his place," I interject in Cain's voice.

She smiles a weak smile. Her eyes roll in the back of her head as a passing labor pain rocks her. "Like old times," she muses through gritted teeth.

"You can do this," he coaches. "Like you've done before."

She holds her breath and bears down. Her cloaca opens a little more with a squishing noise, and she grabs tightly onto my hand squeezing Cain's thick fingers—*my* thick fingers. The head of the creature pokes through.

I reach down to the opening with my free hand—Cain's free hand—and wipe away some of the black ooze. I touch the head, and it's like stone. Like the body of Sataniel in his true form. A fissure opens at the top of the skull, hot lava oozing from it. It drips onto the platform, and Lilith screams when it burns through her delicate opening.

"One more push, beautiful," Cain coaxes. "You're almost there."

And again, she squeezes his hand hard and pushes with all her might. The lifeless creature plops out of her in a sheath of gray casing, and she cries.

I pick up the child and hand it to her. She cradles it close to her chest as the snakes on her head lick it clean. "I will call him Caniel," she says. "Because you helped me."

"You did a good job," Cain says to her.

"Thank you," she says in a muffled voice and hands me the child. "You do it. Please."

I take the child in my arms and fling it into the Lake. The stone structure of its skull splits open and sizzles in the fire. I crouch down low next to Lilith, wrap my arm around her shoulder, and pull her close to my chest. But *I* don't do that. *Cain* does. Lilith nuzzles her head into my chest and brings one of her hands down between my legs. Surprised, my body jolts a little when she tugs at me.

"Will you love me now?" she whispers, and my chest tightens up with anxiety.

"Oh, Lilith! You know I can't. You are the Serpent Queen. You know it doesn't work that way," Cain says, and I relax a little from his response.

She chuckles with a deranged sound and burrows her head deeper into the crook of my arm. "Silly me. I don't know what I was thinking."

Her hot tears stream on my bare chest, and I hold her close a while longer.

## CHAPTER SEVENTEEN

# THE NEW PLAN

After I had cradled Lilith in Cain's arms by the Lake, I pushed him away and went back to my natural shape; however, a speck of his lightning scar remains on the top of my shoulder. Maybe it was always there. I had sucked in the humans and turned my skin gray. I had stolen Revalia's purple haze into my eyes. Perhaps, each one of the souls now resting inside Apophis has manifested themselves back into some physical transformation on my body, like a constant reminder of the souls I have taken. But, I wouldn't know because I haven't paid that close attention. I haven't cared all that much.

When I had changed from Cain back into myself, Lilith was confused at first, rambling about a thief stealing her best friend's face. In her delirium, she hit me and spit at me and tried to set her snakes on me, but she was weak and hysterical and couldn't quite grasp that I was controlling her snakes the entire time. Her frenzy had blinded her to my power over her. When she finally had calmed down, she looked into my eyes and dreamily called me by name. "Aestrangel?" she had said with a drunken-like voice.

"Peace, Lilith. I'm not going to hurt you. I'm going to take you back to Lucifer," I said forcefully, tightening my grip on her wrists to stop her furious onslaught.

"Hmmm..." she huffed with eyes half-closed. "You. And my son."

She waved her finger in the air to show her disapproval of my union with Malek, but I ignored it.

"No, no, no," I disputed falsely. "You're making something out of nothing." Her upper torso was like a mass of jelly in my arms, and she could barely keep herself from toppling over. "I'm after bigger things. More powerful things," I had said, but whether she heard or understood me is a mystery.

Lucifer is back at the throne room when Lilith and I return from the Lake of Fire. I know I must remain on high alert because Malek and Alukah are not here, and I am curious as to what has happened with Orobas, the Oracle. I try my best to stay calm and not appear too suspicious. Lucifer scurries over as we make our way from the corridor, and he throws his arms around Lilith lovingly. It is obvious he is worried about her by the way he speaks gently and the way he grips her elbow, shoos her away from me, and guides her over to her throne. Without the weight of a child inside her, she is much more agile than she was before. Her movements are smoother and quicker, and her size has decreased dramatically. She is able to slither easily unto her bed and curl her long tail under her, and Lucifer kneels beside her, stroking her, showing his undying devotion and affection for her.

"Samael! Samael!" she calls to him, reaching up to his face and running her fingers up and down his cheeks. "I've missed you so much!"

He looks over his shoulder to me. "Did everything go okay?"

I nod to him. "And you?" I say, referring to his excursion to Sheol.

He nods quickly, and I can't get a read on what it's supposed to mean. All I know is Lucifer is here, and Malek and Alukah are not. Did they find something out? Does Lucifer know about Apophis? Was Malek able to protect my secret? Is Malek okay?

"Oh, Samael!" Lilith gushes, breaking my concentration. "You should have seen him. He was beautiful! He would have been strong! He would have cracked open the world and bled it dry!"

He pets her black hair away from her sweat-tinged temples. Her crown of snakes bow their heads to him and drape themselves down the sides of her neck to camouflage their scaly skin within her hair and the folds of the blankets.

"I called him Caniel before we threw him into the Lake. And he burned away to charcoal ash like flash paper igniting in the sky. You like that name, don't you?" she asks frantically.

"Yes, dear," he says trying to calm her down. "I like it very much."

"It's a good name, right? A strong name, don't you think? He would have conquered all at your command, wouldn't he?"

He pets her again. "Yes, Beauty. He would have ruled even me."

She smiles up at him with thankful eyes. He approved, and that's all she wanted to hear.

Yet, I notice a sadness in Lucifer's voice. It's thin and hollow, and I suspect, only reserved for dealing with her. And then I realize... he does this often. *She* does this often. And thus, this is their eternal punishment. *Their* eternal hell.

"I'm so sorry, My Queen," he whispers. "I wanted to be there..."

Her face brightens at the memory. "It's okay. It's okay," she says sweetly with a smile. "You sent Cain in your place. He helped me. Helped the child. He was strong and wonderful like he used to be, and I am so grateful to you for sending him."

Lucifer pulls back in confusion and looks over to me again. I shrug my shoulders in an "I-don't-know" manner and feign confusion as well, keeping my glamouring a well-guarded secret.

"What do you mean?" he asks her.

"Cain," she smiles more widely, crazily. "He was there! At the lake! He said you sent him to be with me. It was a wonderful gesture, and I thank you. You have no idea how much that meant to me."

Lucifer stands up. "Lilith," he says gently. "Cain is gone..."

"Yes, yes," she interrupts. "He stayed with me a little while after but had to leave." She sighs and closes her eyes.

"Okay, okay," he says in a voice to placate the insane. He strokes her hair one last time, tells her to rest, and walks over to me.

His expression speaks volumes.

"Tell me exactly what happened out there," he demands.

I pull back with slight shock at his accusatory tone. "What do you mean?" I scoff in defense.

He tilts his head to the side. "You said everything went well."

"It did. I don't know. She started having visions. No. They were more like hallucinations. She yelled at me at first and didn't want my help, and then she thought I was Cain. It was like her..."

"Her mind split," he finishes.

"I don't know what happened. I didn't encourage it or anything. I just helped her with her... her... process, made sure she was okay, and brought her back here."

He rubs his chiseled chin with his long fingers. "This has happened before," he says in deep thought. "It doesn't happen often, but every once in a while, the madness takes over."

"Madness?"

"I know it's easy to forget, but Lilith was human first. *The* first woman made from the very earth—clay, soil, sand, sea. She was never designed to be a higher being, so when this once strong and defiant ex-wife of Adam challenged both husband and creator and took on a role in the Order of the Daimones, something splintered within her. Humans were never meant to assume the demonic or angelic transformation, and it took her mind some time to adjust. In the beginning, the insanity almost destroyed her, but I was able to gather up the pieces of whatever comforting thoughts and memories she had left, and that's when I created Asphodel. *For her*."

I remember my first time in the strange fog world. I remember Malek's explanation of the realm. He had said: "This is Asphodel, the place of endless dreams. Of endless desires and fantasies. Whatever is in your heart, whatever you want to see or experience is directly at your disposal. Think it, and you can be there." Asphodel was originally the place for Lilith to clear her mind, to straighten out her memories and thoughts, to reconcile her daimon self with her human self. Lucifer's love for Lilith was so great and boundless that he created an entire realm just to save her.

"I'm guessing it worked," I say, but I already know the answer to that.

"You've been there. You know the power of that place. You felt the effects it can have on your mind and on your soul."

I nod, because, yes! Asphodel, for all its foggy ugliness and outlandish creatures that loom in the shadows, is ultimately a world of your own design. It can be whatever you want it to be, and it can show you whatever you want it to show you. It can be a prison of fantasy and reckless abandon or a cage of horrors and nightmares. Whichever you choose, desire, or prefer.

*Horrors... nightmares...* my mind starts to wander into dark territory. An inkling of clarity starts to poke at the front of my skull and at the base of my core. *At Apophis.*

"You sent her there many times?" I ask, probing.

"Like I said, it was hard in the beginning. Lilith often made visits to Asphodel. Part of her healing process was found in the designing of her world itself. She spent countless hours recreating and reconstructing her perfect place. She crafted every detail down to the simplest grains of sand."

"The beach," I say.

"The Land of Nod. Her beach and her cave. Her perfect grotto."

"That's her paradise. And that's why she thought Cain was with her because he was cast to the Land of Nod too. And the two of them were companions, friends."

"Exactly," he confirms. "And while she was building and creating from her memories, she was healing her mind—settling it down in a way. She was rebuilding it so that it could fit in the expansiveness and gravity of her new power and reality."

"You're going to send her back?"

"For a little bit, at least. Again, it's been a long time since she's had an episode, and I'd like to head it off at the pass—before it turns into full-blown mania."

I look over his shoulder and at Lilith on her bed. Her eyes open wide, and she stares directly at me. We lock eyes for a few moments before Apophis kicks from the inside. It kicks through my arms and legs and nearly causes me to stumble forward. I collect myself, straighten up, and smooth my hair down on my chest. "Will she fight you? Will she protest going?"

"Oh no," he says, "she's usually very receptive to the idea. We call it her vacation time. Her sabbatical. Even the most fearsome daimons need a break sometimes." He gives me a sarcastic side-smirk. Is he hinting at the time I spent in Asphodel indulging with Malek? *My* forty days and forty nights of hedonistic pleasure and wanton desire?

"Do you need me to watch over her? I feel like you wanted us to bond and get close, and she and I never really got the chance to on our sojourn to the Lake. I can oversee her in Asphodel if you wish."

He narrows his eyes ever so slightly, like he knows I have ulterior motives but can't be sure of what they are. I smile at him, masking the malice in my words with a jovial and heartfelt expression. "I don't think that will be necessary, Aestrangel, but I appreciate the gesture." He gives a half smile. "You know I will call upon you if needed."

"Of course," I say graciously, and bow my head.

He opens his arms wide. "Come daughter, you always know the right things to say, don't you?"

I step closer and fall into his arms for a fatherly hug. He wraps tightly around me, swooping me into him and enveloping me within his grasp. I squeeze my arms around his waist and hold on for a moment, enjoying the exchange of our auras, basking in the warmth of our familial embrace. Lilith's snakes softly rattle on her head, and she looks over at us with a suspicious eye. His embrace is innocent. The kiss on my forehead is innocent. Nothing more than a father showing affection to his favorite child.

But to Lilith's eyes, to the snakes that watch the world around her and report back to her astral gene, she sees something more. Something darker. Something sinister and of a more mature nature. In her hallucinatory state, in her delusional mind-frame, I flash images of her, not of Lucifer, but of her beloved Samael: Samael bending down and kissing me passionately on the mouth—his hands feverishly moving up and down my body; Samael walking behind me and pushing me to my knees at the stone altar; Samael fanning out my metal wings and fashioning steel bars at my back; Samael mounting me like a demonic lion, grabbing onto my studded bars, and forcing his way inside. "She will bear me a living child, unlike you!" he says to her with venomous anger as I writhe with delight beneath him.

Quickly, she closes her eyes, trying to block out the onslaught of the depraved mirages. Tears begin to stream down her face, and hearing her quiet sobs, Lucifer releases me and goes back to her. I cease the transmission of pictures to poor, weak, Lilith, and her snakes lie back to rest. "Oh, Beauty," he fawns over her, "you know you need to calm yourself down. It's okay now. It's okay."

She jerks away from his touch, haunted by the false visions I emblazoned into her mind.

"Lilith," he says with his palms over her. "It's just me. I'm not going to hurt you."

But she continues to sob into her hands like a child. She can't bring herself to look at him. He thinks he knows why she behaves this way because it's happened before. But, he has no idea.

He walks away from the bed and comes back to me. "I guess it's worse than I thought," he says with a defeated tone. It enrages me so much that I want to stomp the sadness right out of him and toss him into the Lake of Fire along with his dead, useless children. His weakness for her makes me sick. Makes me angry. Makes me want to go on a murderous rampage! Apophis rattles on the inside and I rub my stomach to try to calm the both of us down.

I place my hand on Lucifer's shoulder. "She'll be okay," I say with a fake, hopeful voice. "You said it yourself—this has happened before, and she always pulls through."

With his eyes cast down, he nods slowly. "I know. I know. I just hate seeing her go through it."

"Are you sure you don't want me to go with her to Asphodel? I can stay with her for a little while. I really wouldn't mind."

Lucifer pauses and thinks for a moment before finally closing his eyes and nodding his head.

Herein lies my doorway. My passage. The weak link in the chain. Lilith. I will use Lilith to get to Lucifer. I will use Lilith to my advantage—to rise above and beyond the cosmos.

## CHAPTER EIGHTEEN

# THE FIRST MAN

I'm back at the beach—Lilith's happy place, Lilith's world of memory and fantasy all bundled up into one. Her version of the beach is slightly different from Cain's, but the general construction of the landscape is the same. Asphodel is the place of one's deepest wants and desires, and her version of Nod is bright and sunny. Unlike Cain's sepia skied land, this beach is golden. The hot sun beats down on the white sand beach, but it's not hot underneath my feet. The sand is grainy with crunchy shells to keep it cool. The water is a crystal shade of blue that gently breathes foam-white waves. No dead fish here bobbing wildly amid the whitecaps, no poison liquid lapping on the shore. Beyond the cave, echoes of children's laughter resonates off the rocks, and she smiles when the sound crescendos in time with the cresting waves. Here in her Asphodel, she is human again—strong and confident. Here, she has her human legs, and her caramel-colored skin glistens and glows in the hot sun. Her honey eyes catch the light and reflect the colors of the sea in a spiraling mass of tawny swirls. The only indication of her demonic being is the crown of snakes that dance around her head. She calms them to camouflage within her black tresses, but to the trained eye, they are there—constant reminders that she is, in fact, no longer mortal.

In Lilith's heart of hearts, deep down below the scales and demonic layers, she still has the essence of her original self, and having been the very first human woman to walk the Earth, she has power in and of itself. Unlike the other humans who were bred and born and had their genetic makeup passed down (and muddled) from generation to generation, Lilith was the first! And she was pure. Fashioned from the very soil and sand, her roots to the human realm are still deeply connected. But her design was to be the mother of the people, not of the demonic order. And it makes sense to me now that most demons have an affinity for the humans as well because somewhere in their astral gene they have a sliver of humanity in them—passed down from their ancient Queen Mother. And how would the human race have been different had Lilith stayed the course and fulfilled the expectations of the creator? Both she and her mate were created from the same clay, so would the people they were supposed to create have looked differently, acted differently, sounded differently? I could spend hours on the beach mulling over these minute points, but I have work to do.

She and I sit together at the water's edge in silence. She digs her toes into the sand, curls her knees to her chest, and rests her chin on her knee tops. A look of sheer delight washes over her face as I'm sure she revels in the feeling of human articulation. Her long hair settles behind her in the sand and the snakes curl up around her at the fold of her bottom. To sit here - listening to the waves lap at the shore, hearing the children play merrily in the distance, feeling the full extent of how her body once worked and who she used to be—this is her solace, her "what-could-have-been."

A pulse in my stomach stirs me. It's like a second heart-beat pounding my insides and reverberating up the rest of my body. My metal wings hum from the vibrations, and I close my own eyes to listen deeply. The voices of the throng within are quiet, silent. There's only one sound that is audible to me. One voice. It's not necessarily a voice that speaks words in any one language—to anyone else's ears it would be a rattling cacophony of dissonant sound. But when I pause and fold my essence back into myself and listen, I hear it speak. It's the code of the ancient cosmos, of the purest star-matter, a spark of the Alpha-light from the moment god blinked his eyes and awoke. It's a whisper within, hidden inside a jangling tune.

*Apophis.*

Apophis lets me know that it is time to make my move.

If Lilith submits and calls out to the lord in true sorrow, if she begs for forgiveness from the depths of her heart, would the creator come for her? *Could* the creator forgive her? Would he accept her back into his Kingdom? And what would become of Lucifer? What would become of Gehenna?

*Well, there's only one way to find out...*

I scoop up a handful of sand and let the grains slide through my fingers before clutching them over into a fist. The sounds of children laughing and playing in the distance cease, and with a wave of my forefinger, the sun races across the sky and hangs low on the horizon. A chilly breeze blows in from the sea, and the darkened waves pick up their pace with more furious crashes. Lilith perks up and looks over at me, but I am gone—hidden from her sight, glamoured invisible to her eyes. The snakes at her sides hiss and shake their miniature rattles like baby maracas. They sense my presence—Lilith can too with her preternatural abilities, but she is unsure and confused. She stands up in a daze and heads back to the cave.

Without thinking on it too much, my mind recreates images of the past. Once upon a time, Malek had bestowed the images of Adam and Lilith to me. Images from the dawn of mankind. Their tan skinned bodies shimmered like bronze gods under the midday sun, and their black hair blew in the warm breeze in the Garden of Eternal Summer. They held hands under a fruit tree in a weary attempt to have some affectionate connection, but their faces told a different story. Lilith hated Adam, no doubt about it. Contempt swelled inside her chest when he insisted she have children with him. When she denied him, he was furious with her for breaking the original covenant with the creator. The lord had promised Adam an obedient, subservient wife, and with Lilith, the soil told a different tale.

I follow her back to the cave, ruminating in the memories, recalling the images as best as I can. And as I make my way into the archway of the stone mouth from the shadows of the falling sun, the foot that steps before me is not my own, but a robust hunk of meat—golden and thick with the second toe towering over the big one and a tuft of dark hair blooming in the dead center.

She hears me rustling behind her, turns on her heel, and gasps, "Adam?" when I pass through the shadows and a ray of light catches a glimpse of my ebony hair.

Apophis chose this guise for me, and I will muster up all my masculinity to play the part well. Besides, I had some help from Cain recently, so I'm somewhat familiar with the male form.

"Lilith," I respond and almost shock myself at the deep, gentle voice that comes from my mouth.

Her face twists up, like she recognizes me, but doesn't. Even in her delusional mind that splits between her human and demonic self, she can still sense something is "off" with the Adam before her, but I ignore her curious gestures and continue my way into the cave. The glamour that I have conjured is as good as it's going to get. Besides, even Lilith herself probably doesn't remember the exact likeness of the real First Man, anyway.

"Adam?" she calls again and races up to greet me.

"Yes, Lilith," I say.

She comes about three feet from me and cautiously keeps her distance. "What are you doing here?"

"I always know where to find you," I say, taking a page out of Malek's playbook.

She narrows her eyes at me. "But why now? Why here? You know I don't *want* you to find me, anyway!" she hisses in tune with her snakes.

Even in her fragile mind state, she's going to be a hard one to deal with. The Dark Queen is still a crafty one with semi-wits about her. I will have to handle this very delicately if I am to be successful. But I don't want to be delicate! I don't want to dance around her with subterfuge! I want to sneak up behind her and twist her arm behind her back. I want to pull back her hair and expose her neck! I want to wrap my metal wings around her and slice her to ribbons so that the front of her opened neck sprays her blood over the flayed bodies of her hair snakes! I want to...

Apophis rumbles and I readjust my focus.

"I know," I say as Adam with the same level of vitriol. "But you knew a time would come when we would meet again, wife."

"I'm not your wife. Never was your wife!"

"But you were *supposed* to be," I say waving a hand in the air like a carnival magician. A glittery wave passes in front of her face, and her eyes go wide when she looks inside the smoky dust. There, I project the image of the Garden of Eden in its infancy—untouched and unspoiled by humanity. A blustery storm soaks the earth into muddy puddles as ghostly hands from the sky reach down and play with the brown clay. Slowly, the shapes take form, and the wind blows life into the man and woman—Adam and Lilith. In my head, that's how I see it, and in the glitter fog, I present it as truth. The glow from Lilith's eyes lead me to believe she accepts it as such.

She blinks rapidly, and I fold the image back up into my palms. "I knew we could be so much more. That I could be so much more," she says in a faraway voice.

"And had you just stayed the course, had you just done what you were told to do," I wave my hand again and show her the memory of their fight—the day she left Eden for the beach, "you would not have all this…" I pivot my head around to the structures on the walls and ceilings. The shrines built of the bones of her dead children.

She stiffens up defensively and glares hard at me.

"Look around you!" I yell. "Look around at the horrors that were created from your design! You alone! Your actions! Your sins! Your disobedience! And for what? A temple made from the backs of your dead progeny? Is that all you must show for what you've done? Is this truly something you strive to be proud of? Are you to say that a lifetime with me would have been worse than *this*?" I snap my fingers, and in the distance, the laughter of the children comes back and fills the cavern. She inhales deeply and closes her eyes listening to the melodic sounds of echoes layering the eons. "They could have been yours!" I taunt, and with another snap of my fingers, I plunge us into silence again. Quickly, she opens her eyes, and there's a flash of her old defiance, but it's clouded with the heavy weight of guilt.

"Why have you come here, Adam?" she says, holding back the tears in her eyes.

"Repent, Lilith. God, our father, will forgive you and all your transgressions."

She stands strong for another moment, but she wavers ... she crumbles. Lilith falls to her knees, puts her face in her hands, and weeps. "Samael is my one true thing!"

"Samael? You mean, Lucifer, the Morning Star, Sataniel, the Deceiver, the Prince of Lies, the Dark Lord, He Who Holds the Lightning Rod? The Devil of Devils?"

Then, I remember my time hanging from the cross in The Second Heaven, and I use the words the Great Teacher tried to use on me: "Why can't you open your human heart? Honor your father so that you may live long in the land the lord, your god, gives to you," I say. "All these things he will give you if you fall and repent. If you dedicate yourself to a penitent life and dedicate yourself to the lord, your god, you will be forgiven and at peace."

"No!" she objects. "I will not repent! I have nothing to repent for!" She looks up at me with a tear-stained face. Her hatred of Adam is undeniable. "He breathed his life into us with the promise of free will. And when I exercised that right, it angered you." She rises up and points her slender finger in the center of my chest. "And he didn't like your anger. An unintended consequence, I guess. Anger is merely a by-product of the failure of expectation."

She's good. Even in her delirium, she has such clear and focused insight. Through time and space, she can still see Adam and the creator as the ultimate manipulators they are. A part of me envies her clarity and the strength of her resolve even in the throes of her madness.

"But what about the innocent ones? The ones who sprang from your womb, only to have their breath stolen upon arrival? What about them? What about their lives and free will?" I say and reach for her hand and guide her back out to the beach.

The moonlight glints off the rolling waves, and I clench my fist. I'm going to have to flex my muscle a little harder this time. In Cain's Asphodel, there were dead fish glittering the surface of the poison water on a red tide. *I can do better...*

"Look," I say, pointing out to the black horizon. "The motherless ones cry for you, for they are yours yet not. Unguided and hanging in the balance of the cosmos. You put them there. You damned them to oblivion!"

The waves swell up to monstrous heights, and the white foamy caps tumble not with the salty ocean water but with the tiny bodies of those she never got to love. Thousands upon thousands of dead babies bob up and down and wash up along the shore. Shells and seaweed and fetal-positioned slabs of meat come in with the angry tide.

Lilith cries out, "No! No! Not here! They're not supposed to be here! This is my place! My place!"

"This is all of them, Lilith!" I say. "Thousands upon thousands that you allowed to suffer and die all because you needed your free will. All because you were tempted by the demon. How many more of your children will have to die? If you repent, you will be reunited with them in paradise! Be a mother to them, Lilith. Let the guilt and sorrow into your heart, and all will be set right in the world."

She flings her body into the sea and lets the waves pull her out up to her waist. Frantically, she tries to scoop the little bodies into her arms and pulls them close to her chest, crying and apologizing to each one of them. It's pathetic to watch as she picks up a child, calls it by name, and cradles it as if it were still alive. And she cries out in agony when a wave topples her over and snatches the body out of her grasp.

"Adam!" she wails from the depths of her lungs and the pit of her stomach. "Adam!" she grunts as she trudges out from the grip of the ocean's current. She's dripping on the beach, her hair snakes poised at attention.

I extend my hand to help keep her steady, but she crumbles to the sand at my feet, her hair wrapping around my ankles like an onyx blanket. I breathe in, knowing this could be it! This could be the moment I've been waiting for! "Lilith!" I say with my deepest, most booming Adam voice, "Do you repent?"

She turns her head up and looks at me with her desperate, crazy eyes. Apophis flutters on the inside, and my excitement rises so much I can barely keep the mask of my Adam Glamour intact. I feel my aura flashing in and out of reality—my lights sparkling to Aestrangel, Adam, Apophis, Aestrangel, Adam, Apophis. But Lilith doesn't seem to notice. Under her arm, a baby foot pokes out. She's held onto to this particular baby so tightly that the body has become nothing but a gelatinous sack.

She opens her mouth to speak, but before the words make their way across her lips, someone shouts my name from the mouth of the cave.



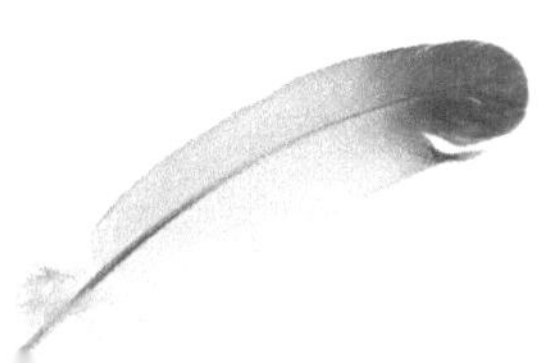

# THE DECEPTION

The outline of a dark angel with extended wings looms in the opening of the passageway. The shape of a beautiful black cross with ebony feathers catching the moonlight's rays stands steadfast in a fixed position. It towers high above the opening like the crucifix at Golgotha casting a moon-shadow on the white sand beach. "Aestrangel!" the voice calls again. It's honeyed and sweet, but desperate and hollow at the same time.

"Malek," I sigh, and the Adam Glamour fades away. I am left in my Aestrangel shell with my black hair blowing sideways with the wind. Lilith's trance disintegrates, and she curls into a ball at my feet and rocks back and forth, mumbling unintelligibly to herself.

I race up the beach to meet him. His face is like chiseled stone with his jaw pushing forward and the hard lines of his cheekbones jutting out from the sides of his face. "W... What are you doing here?"

"You know I always know where to find you," he says matter-of-factly. The absence of his charming smile unnerves me.

"Yes, but..."

"But what are *you* doing here?" he presses.

I slouch my body to the side and huff like a sassy teenager. He and I can always relate to the human mannerisms we possess, and I do this gesture in hopes of breaking his stony glare. But it doesn't work. He remains unwavering in his stance, barely looking at me. "You know why I'm here. You know what needs to be done."

His eyes remain focused straight ahead, fixed on the curled-up body of Lilith on the beach. For a second, the side of his mouth twitches downward in a knowing way, but he quickly straightens it out. "But, she's my mother," he says softly, so softly that I can barely hear him.

I fan my wings out with a thunderous clang so that I can match the outline of his shape and we are lined up in perfect synch. My wings are stronger, thicker, and they obstruct his vision of Lilith. We stand face to face, wingspan to wingspan. The moonlight reflects off my wings and bounces back at him, casting eerie, jagged shadows over his face. I reach for his chin and force his gaze to me, force his eyes to stare into mine. "Look at me!" I command, and with a slow roll, he glides his eyes directly at mine. His stormy gray eyes are silent and sad—no maelstrom swirling, no tsunami eating small islands, not even a serene woodland field with grazing animals. Nothing. I can't even see my own reflection within them. My heart sinks a little because Malek's eyes have always been a safe place for me. "You know what I have to do," I repeat more firmly, more authoritatively.

"Like this?" he asks, and I feel so sorry for him. "By torturing her?"

"Don't pretend you're above torture. Don't pretend you're above deception. Do you have any other solutions or suggestions?"

He closes his eyes with a slight shake of his head. "This will destroy her. This will change everything."

I hold his face firmly in my hand. My aura screams to him, but he has shut me out, and for the first time since I've met him, I can't hear his low-rumbling hum—the natural magnetic vibration that comes from deep within him. I start to panic. My hands can't keep steady. Malek is my constant, my cornerstone. I can't do this without him. I don't want to do this without him. "Look at me," I implore. "Let me show you what I see."

Because I want to show him. I want to secretly show him the full extent of my plan and my perceived outcomes. I want to *show* him what I want, but I can't do that unless he looks at me.

"I understand your conflict," I say. "I do. Truly. I understand that tug on the inside between your parental loyalty and your own wants and desires. I had a mother once too. And although she was counterfeit, at the time, she was real. She was real to someone, somewhere far-far away. And you know what's at stake here. Please, Malek," I beg from the deepest part of my heart. "Please look at me."

Slowly, he opens his eyes with a look of sheer hatred and contempt, but I ignore it and strengthen my grip on his chin.

"They're going to take me away," I plead through gritted teeth. "They're going to nail me back on that cross and poke and prod me until there's nothing left. They're going to find Apophis and do God-knows-what with it.

There will be nothing left of me!" I feel hot tears rise into the bottom of my eyelids.

He knows what I say is true. His feathers stiffen at the thought of my destruction, and I think his stomach does a flip-flop or two, but he recovers and says coldly, "You're not their objective anymore."

I huff. "You're not that naïve. You and I both know I've been their main objective since I killed Camael. They may have shifted their strategy, but we know what they're after."

He rolls his eyes knowingly.

"And I don't trust the Morning Star. If it comes down to him or me..."

He raises his finger and places it on my lips to silence me, and suddenly, I realize we are in Lilith's Asphodel, and not our own. We could possibly be heard here.

Like a light switch turning on, I hear his electric hum return. "Show me," he says into my head. "Show me everything you want."

"And you?" I say back telepathically. "I want to know what you want."

"I know I don't want you to end up as their little astral experiment!"

"Oh, is that all?" I use my inner human sarcasm.

He smiles at me and tilts his head forward, and there he is! There's my Malek! My charming, dashing, devilish Malek. The king of my strange, demonic heart. With both hands, he takes my face and brings us forehead to forehead. I grip my hands around his wrists as he holds my face in place. And we stare. We stare at each other and allow ourselves to travel out and in and between and up and down. We're in his woodland field with the gray sky, but we're in my violet patch of crying lilies and chrysanthemums. We're on the beach, but we're in the Brooklyn brownstone. We're in the darkest cavern of Gehenna, but we're in a tent in a valley of the Grand Canyon. We're nowhere and everywhere, and it takes a moment to figure out the balance of time and space between us.

Then we're in the great void. A chasm of black silence. Aestrangel and Malek. Humans and Angels and Demons and strangeness and perfection and horror and horns and hooves and wings and metal and feathers all hanging, dangling in the vast expanse. Queen and King. Absolute deities of anger, deception, violence, vengeance, illusion, manipulation, and *dominance*. We are beautiful, he and I—a conglomeration of all the good parts and all the bad parts of all of creation. And in this space of nothingness and timelessness, it manifests so clearly—we want the same things. What swirls in his heart and soul is the exact complement to what bounds in my own. A sharp whisper inside tells me that it always has been and always will be.

"To reign supreme," I whisper.

He pulls his hands away, releasing me, and I step back. We're still on the beach at the opening of the cave. The waves crash all around us, and we breathe in the salty, acrid air. "But it's yours," he says out loud. "It's always been yours. I don't want it. You will fashion the new world how you like. I will be here merely to help you, to guide you, to advise you, to hold you in our Asphodel in complete and utter decadence."

My face twists in confusion, and I fold my wings against my back. He reaches for my hands and grips them tightly. "But we just..."

He collapses his wings as well. "No," he assures. "I want you. All of it, yes. All of you, yes. But the crown is for you and you alone."

I look back to Lilith squirming in the sand—a helpless mass of rattling snakes and a mind full of wicked delirium. "She won't recover this time if you let me do this."

"I know."

"With Lilith gone, there's no telling how he will react," I say, referencing the Morning Star.

I sense the rise and fall of his head in a solemn nod. "I know. And I know you're willing to take that chance."

He's right. I'm at my window of opportunity. The knocking on the door is deafening. This is the precipice of the nevertime—because this is the now or the never, and I can't accept anything less than the now. I scoff at the never. Besides, I won't even have a never if I don't act now!

"Will you stay here when I do what I need to do?"

He hesitates for a second. "How can I not? I have an obligation to be here—for you … and for her."

I nod. I can feel his conflicted weight hanging heavy in the space around us. Torn between his own wants and desires, torn between his feelings for me, torn between his strange obligation of being a son, Malek wrestles internally with what needs to happen. I can't fault him for it either. Just as I am the strange angel, Malek is the strange demon in his own right—tainted with his own shard of humanity. Because of it, he is the only one of Lilith's progeny who has an ounce of dedication to her, and to witness her destruction must give him a twinge of pain. Not the level of suffering the Angelos felt when they lost their very own Camael, but something deep enough to stir him and throw him off balance.

However, the prospect of my destruction outweighs the prospect of hers, and this is why I know he will be my most esteemed General when I rise to power. He and I will work hand in hand, side by side, in perfect syncopated rhythm, because I know how he feels about me. I know he has dreams of a little black haired boy with gray eyes and silver feathered wings running between my legs and hiding from Malek's stony cloven hooves in a game of hide-and-seek.

I continue to stare at Lilith writhing in a pile of tiny bodies that have washed up on the shore. "Will you hate me for it when it's done?"

He inhales loudly. "Perhaps."

Apophis kicks at me because it knows Malek is not being entirely truthful. A day will come when... "You *will* want it for yourself, though. One day." I turn to face him, and it's written all over him—in his posture, expressions, and gestures. This could very well be the one defining moment that drives us apart and returns us back to being adversaries like we were in the beginning. But right now, standing before me, he is Malek. He is *mine*. A vision of horrific beauty and grace who hums to my astral soul with deep, rhythmic pulses. I marvel at his image—breathe in his essence, realizing he was the one soul I did not consume an ounce of. I kept him pure and guarded and safe and refused to steal of his essence because he is my equal.

*Until he's not.*

"One day you will want to fashion this world for *your* liking," I say with a foreboding tone.

"But that day is not today," he says in a soothing voice, and a side grin creeps at the edge of his mouth because *he knows*. He knows where we stand in this moment. In the now. He knows no matter what he says or how he protests, I am going to obliterate Lilith, his mother, one way or another. He knows I will reign, and he will assist. And he knows he will one day form plans and plots of his own.

I extend my hand to him. "Coming?"

He folds his arms across his muscular chest—the chest of man and beast and human and demon. "No. I'll stay right here. This is all you."

I pull my hand away and place my arms down at my sides. "Are you sure?" I ask again.

"Yes, Aestrangel. Do what needs to be done. It's okay."

I want to say so much to him, to explain my rationale, to verbally outline my intentions and motivations, but *he knows*. I must keep reminding myself of that. Malek knows and understands, and in a weird, demonic way, he gave me his wicked blessing. Apophis wiggles with excitement, and uncontrollably, my wings clumsily flail out behind me. I don't like the feeling of not being in control, and my concern for how much longer I can hold on to Apophis as it grows. I hear rustling behind me and turn to look back. Malek has extended his wings once more, and as I walk farther away, his shape looks like the cross on the Golgotha hill again like an omen, a warning of sorts. Apophis shivers, echoing my own thoughts.

I continue my walk back to the beach. The moon seems to follow me like a spotlight glinting off my metal wings, creating a path in front of me along the white sand. Lilith is on her side, rocking back and forth, and when I reach her, I kneel down and attempt to pet her hair. Immediately, her snakes rise up and hiss at me in unison, but with a simple flick of my finger, they are lulled into submission. I extend my hand to them, and they gather close to me, flitting their forked tongues to my heat signature and rattling their tails like puppies wagging happily for their master. I am their master. The empty shell of a deranged demon no longer controls them.

I tap Lilith's shoulder, and she is startled at my touch. "Aestrangel?" she questions, her voice high-pitched and

erratic. "Where's Adam? Where are the children? Where is Samael?"

I scoot my body closer to her and guide her head into my lap. "Shhh," I say stroking her hair and curling the thin snake bodies around my fingers. "Relax, Lilith. It will all be over soon."

CHAPTER TWENTY

## THE CONFRONTATION

Just when I think I can have a moment of uninterrupted peace to do my work, to release Lilith from her demonic shackles and her insanity laden existence, the clouds in the sky gather fiercely and rumble the realm with a deep-throttle thunder. A thick bolt of purple lightning strikes the surface of the sea and sends a violet, electric glow across the horizon. Another flash splits a seam open in the sky, and a swirling vortex grows in the center of the atmosphere. The gaping hole twists and turns violently like a sideways tornado. A wave of red smoke slowly filters from the opening, and I stand up to watch the interruption unfold as Lilith lies still in the sand.

Alukah floats down from the dark heavens—her black hood covers her kaleidoscope face. As she glides across the choppy waves to meet me, the bottom of her robe dips into the salty water. I look over my shoulder to see if Malek is still at the cave. He is—set firmly in his crossed

-199-

arm position with his wings fanned out. I mimic his pose and cross my arms over my chest defensively. I know he will stay and observe. I know he will only intervene if I need him.

But I won't need him.

I knew a confrontation with Alukah was going to be in my future; I just wasn't sure when that future would be the present. Well, I guess there's no time like the...

After our encounter in the Black Keep—after she ripped my feathers right off my bones, then pulverized the bones into ash and dust, neutered me like a helpless alley cat—I vowed she and I would come face to face again. I'm conflicted though. I am very curious as to why she's come to Lilith's Asphodel. How did she know I was here? Does she know what I plan to do? Did she come to save her mother, like Malek had attempted? My curiosity will certainly get the best of me. My curiosity might very well end up being the end of me. What's that old human saying? Curiosity killed the cat? Alukah knows not the extent of my power. Her presence here tells me that *she* is the curious one...

Every step she takes is like a colored strobe light flashing rapidly around her. She doesn't move with a graceful gait like an angel, or a stomping, shifting move-ment of a daimon. She flickers in and out of reality that is barely noticeable to the naked eye. But I notice it. I notice her flutterby movements so acutely that it makes me dizzy if I stare too long.

I look at her and point over my shoulder to Malek at the cave. "You and your brother are fabulous trackers," I say, the sarcasm dripping from my tongue.

She gives something like a crackled cackle. "Your blood is hard to ignore," she growls with her ice-crunching voice.

*A sentence without a riddle. We're making progress.*

I fan out my wings with a loud metallic clang to show her how much I've grown. She removes her hood revealing her digitized face is frozen in the "oh" position for a few seconds before going back to the continuous stream of jerky-motioned expressions.

"And so, to what do I owe the pleasure of your company?" I say as I gently rattle my blades.

She smiles, or what seems like a smile for her clown face. All that I can truly make out in the chaotic flashes are her fangs hanging low beyond her pixelated lips. "I had to be sure, I said. I had to know for myself, I said. No, we said. No, she said," she chants with three different distinct voices. I guess I spoke too soon. I guess I will have to endure the sing-song enigmas she is known to dole out, at least for a little while longer. I can't help but pick up on the timbre of excitement in her multiple tones, as if she can barely contain herself or subdue the forces that reside within her. But my forces are stronger. Apophis shimmies, tickling the edge of my spine and I shift from one foot to the next.

"Be sure of what?" I probe.

Alukah blinks crazily and begins to circle around me, being cautious not to step inside my striking range. My wings are wide, menacing, powerful, and deadly. This much she knows. She is wise not to get too close when I am opened up like this.

"Mother, mother, on the floor. Who's the sanest of them all? Before me stands Gehenna's Whore. Waiting on a distant shore."

I arch my back slightly as my feather blades tilt horizontally ready for an attack. "Watch your tongue," I admonish.

She gives another crackly laugh. "Do you mean this one?" she says with the voice of a human woman and quickly extends her tongue in my direction. It's black and forked and dangles in front of her face down to the center of her chest. Green and yellow pustules explode like tiny volcanoes, and their ooze seeps into little toxic pools in the sand. She slurps it back in and laughs again.

"What did you need to be sure of?" I repeat, trying to wash away the vile image from my mind.

"We knew! We knew! We knew about you!" She continues to dance around me clapping her hands. "But you hide! You hide! You hide so well! Strange indeed. Strange alas!"

I narrow my eyes and look over to Malek who has remained in place. He gives me no sign of understanding and no inkling of guidance. "What do I hide?" I say nonchalantly. "What is it you think you know?"

"Orobas, the Oracle, the seer of the deep. The one who drank the sacred blood of secrets we should keep. Power, power great and wide is locked tight deep within. And glamoured, glamoured at your side, of all the souls again."

The picture starts to become clear, starts to paint itself among her grating words. I breathe in, maintaining my composure. "When you healed me," I say, "you drank my blood."

She stops in front of me and sighs at the memory. The sound is like jagged nails across rusty metal. "So sweet, so sweet. A tasty treat, a tasty treat." The variants of smiles on her face flash dynamically—so quickly that her visage is a blob of pink for a few moments, like a hunk of salmon-colored cotton candy from her crazy carnival.

"And the Oracle?" I continue, piecing it all together. "You visited him, and *he* drank from *you*."

She claps her hands together excitedly again. "We found you! We found you!" she cheers with the creepy baby doll aspect of herself. "And he said unto me, 'The waters which thou sawest, where the whore sitteth, are peoples, and multitudes, and nations, and tongues.'" She quotes Scripture, one of her favorite things to do.

"Orobas said this to you?"

She lowers her face and bends over slightly. Looking up at me with her fixed eyes, she points to my chest and snarls, "No. *He* did."

*Apophis.*

She knows not his name, but she is aware of his existence. I take a step backward to get out of her reach. Malek's feathers rustle behind me—I can hear the panic in them as the sound is carried on the ocean breeze.

"Peoples, and multitudes, and nations, and tongues, peoples, and multitudes, and nations, and tongues, peoples and multitudes, and nations, and tongues." She repeats over and over—slowly at first, then faster and faster and faster, until the words are garbled and jumbled and a chaotic mess of nonsense.

I steady myself and run various exit strategies and cover-ups through my mind. "What is it you think you know?" I scoff.

"You are an architect, Mother Harlot," she hisses. "But no weapon formed against us will prosper, and every tongue which rises against us in judgment, we shall condemn."

Every tongue. She means all those I have consumed—angel, demon, human. So many I've lost count. So many, I could raise nations with their essence. So many, I could raze nations with their aura. Apophis stirs at the threat, the direct affront to his being. I widen my stance and tilt my feather blades a little more. My black hair blows in swirls around my head, and I extend my arms at my sides. "Weapon? So, Lucifer sent *you*? To do what? Disarm me?"

She twitters and jitters. The Maiden, Mother, and Crone fight for dominance on her face. There is a second of guilt and confusion for each one had something to say but was hesitant to speak.

"You're just his seer, Alukah. His servant. And now you come to act as his colonel?"

With my mind, I tap inside her psyche, swirling with the voices, riding on the circle of chaos in her head. "He doesn't know... I didn't disobey... He was preoccupied... I wanted to make him proud... I needed to confirm... I needed to... I wanted to... I had to..." all the voices yell at once.

I raise my hand and fold my fingers up into a fist. Immediately, Alukah's brain voices are silenced, and she looks at me wide-eyed in terror. Her rotating face stops with a fixed mouth hanging agape.

"Lucifer didn't send you," I say, repeating what I heard in her head. "So, why did you come here? To stop me? Or do you have your own agenda? Oh, perhaps you do."

My words poke at her, make her falter slightly. Her shoulders dip forward as she takes in what I said. But I know the truth. She has come straight from Orobas to save her mother and curry favor with her father by exposing me. Exposing my secret. Exposing Apophis.

She doesn't answer, so I dart my pointer finger in the air with a sideways motion. She stumbles onto one knee in the sand but quickly rights herself, stands straight up at attention, and is propelled from the ground in a cloud of red smoke. "Protect the Father," she sings. "Protect the

Mother," and Lilith sits up in the sand to gaze upon her child with eyes of awe and wonder.

"Alukah?" she whispers in a daze.

Alukah looks down at her mother, and her face stops at one of a pained expression. The look of worry and concern darkens her, and it looks as if tears are welling in the corners of her eyes.

*Demons don't cry. Demons don't cry.*

Lilith reaches out her hand to Alukah gesturing for help. She nods at her mother in acknowledgment and turns her circus face back to me. "What have you done, bastard of the sun?" she spits. "Drunken with the blood of the saints and blood of the martyrs. Did you think you would infiltrate us at our core? Traitor in our midst. Destroyer in our path." The red smoke carries her high above me. "No longer sixty-six inside, but many more. So much more. Deceive the Deceiver, a perilous feat."

She waves her arms in the air, and the red smoke billows at her feet and creeps its way over to me. It encircles me from the bottom up, holding my legs in place, paralyzing me where I stand. Her power is strong; her magic is dense. My blades shudder against each other like tinkling bells as I try to dislodge myself, try to wriggle free of her hold. And I remember her words. I remember the day she tore my feathers from me. She had held me in place much like this, and she tortured me. Quill by quill by quill. And her stupid rhymes of numbers and jokes were all a game to startle and confuse me. I cannot allow her to use her power over me again. I vowed to make her pay. Vowed to make her suffer for what she did to me.

*And I love to keep my promises.*

Apophis jerks forward inside me with such great force that I stumble forward into the sand. Alukah gasps, a muddled sound of disbelief that I have freed myself from her shackles. I shoot up into the air and meet her where she hovers. She hides her face from me under her hood.

"You stole from me," I say. "But I rose up to become something new, something better." I clang my blades together, deafening the realm. "And you said I couldn't create life, but you were wrong. You can feel the energy churning in me! It grows every day. Every moment."

"Speak not, Aestrangel. Your boasting and pride will tear you asunder!" she screams, and the soundwaves of her voice form a white wave that sends me flying.

I arch my back to halt my tumble, catch the wind within the steel of my wings, and thrust myself back to where she hovers.

"Does he know?" I scream. "Does Malek know what Orobas told you?"

She shakes her head.

"Does the Morning Star know what Orobas told you?"

She laughs again—low and sinister. "The Morning Star knows everything. He knows the past, present, and future. And he knows beyond what you can fathom. He's seen into the cosmos. He knows where your fate takes you. Here. On this beach. With me."

I try to keep from snickering. If Lucifer's taught his daughter anything, it's to whole-heartedly believe the lies that come out of her own mouth because she spouts out insanity with the sanest of tones. She believes herself. She believes in herself. And in her eyes, her father is pure, true, and good. It's rather pathetic if you ask me. "You're as delusional as your mother," I growl, and Alukah's attention drifts downward to Lilith on the beach. "I've surpassed you. I've surpassed all of Gehenna! You will not steal anything from me ever again!"

"If you are as powerful and mighty as you claim to be, I'm curious to see how you crash into the sea!" She sings and laughs and sings and laughs and sings and laughs.

In an instant, I fold my wings forward, blades straight ahead at my sides, and I descend a few feet below Alukah in the air. I point my toes downward and race through the sky with one, swift upward lift.

I cut straight up and through Alukah's body with my wings. The feather blades slice through the soles of her feet and split each leg in half causing her body to fold outward like flower petals opening wide to greet the summer sun and the dewy morning—the three sections of her topple over and fall to the beach like the soft shavings of a wooden log. When each piece of her hits the sand, the bodies transform before my eyes. There they are—the Maiden with her long platinum hair and soft supple skin positioned like Sleeping Beauty in a deep slumber; the Mother with her golden curls framing her face and shoulders and her distended stomach protruding with life that could never be; and the Crone with her hair grayed from age and her ashen colored skin set deep with the ancient lines of time. Their faces are their own now—no longer do they fight for dominance in Alukah's body. No longer do they strive for control. Their voices are quieted in eternal sleep, and they are at peace.

I lay myself into a horizontal position and float over the three bodies on the shoreline. Apophis rattles me with excitement. I feel his hands groping at the soft spots of my insides, clawing at my underside like a magnet trying to reach its opposite pole. He reaches for her—Alukah. Reaches with his little hands to draw in the lingering powers of the Maiden, Mother, and Crone before they dissipate into Asphodel's Oblivion. But his hands aren't so little anymore, and he practically drags me down unto the dead bodies. Quickly, I try to jerk away, but he tugs so hard, I can't help but stagger in mid-air.

When he finally gets a hold on their astral openings, he sucks in their auras with a deep inhale and holds them in the center of my chest squirming and bucking around to make room for their magnanimous spirit.

The new influx weighs me down, and I roll onto my back on the shore. I dig my toes into the sand and let the new sensation pull on me, drag my body into the grains, sink into the Asphodel terrain. Malek swoops down by my side and cradles my head in his hands. I can barely manage to open my eyes to look at him.

"You can't hold it in much longer, can you?" he says, but it's more of a statement than a question. His voice sounds like echoes of transmitter static.

A strobing sensation creeps up around me, and I feel as if I'm flickering in and out of reality, much like how Alukah did. Second to second I blink in the darkness and beach, darkness, and beach. I'm afraid I'm going to lose myself to the Oblivion if I don't figure out a way to expel Apophis from me. He will consume me to nothing, and while the Angelos and Daimones will have both lost, I will have lost too, leaving nothing but the pure matter of Apophis in my stead. And I can't let that happen. I can't have come all this way to fold up inside myself and become something else.

I am Aestrangel. And failure is not an option.

"You haven't failed, though," Malek whispers, and I realize I must have been mumbling my inner thoughts out loud. "You have one more thing to do. Do you think you can do it?" he says in a voice that cheers me on. A voice that is like a human giving encouragement to a teammate or friend in need.

I lift my head up from his lap and scan the beach. Lilith has crawled to the remains of Alukah and has thrown her body across her corpses. She wails and flails and cries out from the depths of her mother's sorrowful and mourning heart. I look up to Malek, and he nods at me.

"Yes. Yes, I can do this," I say as I pull myself up and crawl over to her.

# CHAPTER TWENTY-ONE

# THE END

"Lilith," I whisper when I get close enough to her. "Lilith. It's okay. Why do you cry, Ancient Queen?" My voice is calm and soothing. I exhibit much control, but really, I feel like there is none in me. My insides rumble and jumble, Apophis sputtering around like a motorized wheel. I find it hard to concentrate, and it takes everything in my power to relax myself and focus. Lilith looks over to me with her tear-stained face. Her eyes are red and puffy, and there's a sadness written all over her—like she's had enough. Like she's done. She just needs a little more guidance to finalize her decision.

I prop myself up on my knees and point to the corpses. "Tell me, Mother of the Night, who is the receiver of you tears?"

Lilith looks over the three bodies with sorrow.

"Demons don't cry," I say in a low, sarcastic voice. "You probably should stop, ya know?"

She's too distraught to notice my malicious undertones, though. She moves her head frantically around scanning the beach, the bodies, me, Malek, and a wave of terror washes over her. "I... I... I'm not a demon," she says bewilderedly.

I cock my head to the side and pout out my lower lip. "Of course you are! Not only are *you* a demon, but you have mothered many. There," I point over and look to Malek, "that is your son, Malek Forcas. He is an esteemed Prince of Gehenna who commands legions! He is wonderful!" I gush and smile brightly (as brightly as I can muster). "He is loyal and obedient and will do anything to protect those he cares about, but he is also cunning and crafty with power beyond compare! He is one of your more perfect creations."

"Malek?" she mouths his name as if trying to spring forth a memory. She stares at him for some time until the veil of confusion lifts from her eyes and she sees him with her mother's heart. "Oh, Malek!" she finally says when a piece of her recognizes him. "My son?" she questions as she continues to wrestle herself in her mind. "But... but... I'm not a demon!" she insists.

"But you are," I say and wave my hand over her to show her a glimpse of her true self. Her human legs temporarily transform back into her snake tail, and her eyes go wide with horror when the tail appears then flashes away back to legs. It's the legs that are the glamouring and the snake tail that is the reality. I just lifted the illusion for a second or two.

"Nod. Samael. Cain," she mumbles.

"That's right," I confirm for her and then point to the three bodies. "And this? Do you know who this is? The seer? The vampire? The Maiden, Mother, and Crone?"

She gets on her knees and looks to each one, studying the faces, moving her hands over the outline of the bodies. Finally, she closes her eyes and whispers sadly, "Alukah."

"Yes," I say, "Alukah. Your daughter. She is no more. How many more of your children must die, Lilith?" I reach over to her and put my hand on her shoulder. I fight the fading feeling in my head and tell Apophis to calm down. Lilith's snakes dip to my hand to greet me. Their little forked tongues flick at my fingers, and with my mind, I tell them to be still. They obey my command, retreat up to the top of her head and nestle like a crown amidst her black hair. "For ages you have suffered," I continue. "Suffered so much loss and heartache. Your love for Samael runs so deep, but what about you?" I touch the center of her chest. "How much more can you take? Eternity is too long, Lilith," I pause, "even for Lucifer."

Her jet-black eyes darken, and she looks up at me under her hooded lids. She recognizes me now. She remembers the false visions I showed her of me and her dear Samael in the throes of unbridled passion, and a tumult of jealousy begins to swell up inside of her. "You," she growls under her breath.

"You've felt it. You've seen it. You've known for a while now. You knew it was coming. You once told me that it was *you* who chose Samael, but now *he* has chosen me. His dedication to you could only last if he needed you. And now he doesn't. You can't give him what he wants because you are cursed—cursed from the Creator and cursed in your humanity. I am the more suitable mate for him. You knew that from the moment I stepped foot in the throne room, and now, well, it's all coming to fruition. He has chosen me to replace you."

She hangs her head down between her knees in defeat. "But I've given him everything he wanted!" she wails in agony.

"One every century? Surely you can't think that is enough when I can populate his army one hundred times as fast—when I can produce for him the child who can pierce the very heart of Ilarium." She puts her head in her hands, and the tears soak through her fingers and into the sand. The moonlight catches the reflection of her liquid pain. "Lilith, isn't it about time you've started thinking about your own path? How long has it been? You were merely a youngling when you left Adam—barely able to see the world and all its treasures with your newborn eyes." I run my hand up and down her back to soothe her, and the snakes assist me with a low, gentle rattle of their tails. "You scarcely got to feel the love and serenity from the creator. You left Eden in such a hurry and sequestered yourself here in Nod. And the creator's love and devotion had a snippet of a second to infiltrate your heart. But it's still there. I promise you. You can still feel it if you wish to. You can let the lord's light and mercy lift you up and carry you off into an eternity of peace and harmony. It's so wonderful! Being in his presence, being free of any obligations and pain and having nothing but purity and love to fill you up is something you have never experienced. But you *can* experience it!"

She lifts her head from her hands and turns toward me.

"No more pain. No more loss. He will forgive you if you have true sorrow in your heart. He will accept your apology if you make one in earnest. And you will be free!" I extend my arm out in front of me in a semi-circular motion, making the bodies of the dead babies disappear from the shore and the water. There is nothing but the clear, clean ocean with the spotlight of the full moon beating down on its serene surface. "No longer would you have to endure year after year of death."

Apophis shakes inside me, and I sway for a second. I can right myself back into a kneeling position before I tumble over.

"Free?" she mumbles.

"Yes, Lilith," I say with an affirming tone. "You can be free. No longer daimon, but pure spirit. Pure light. No longer will you have the struggle within your mind, either."

Suddenly, Alukah's demon bodies disintegrate and turn to ash, and we both watch as their final remnants blow out onto the open water. I turn my attention to Malek, but he's no longer on the beach, no longer in this realm of Lilith's Asphodel. I guess he couldn't stand to watch the destruction of his mother. Or her salvation. Or neither. I have no idea what will happen to her when I am finished. Will the creator really forgive her for eons of rebellion? I don't know, and I don't care.

Lilith sighs. Deep, heavy, and contemplative.

I wave my hand in front of her face, sending her images of what I imagine her life to be. "You can be whole, Lilith. Something you never truly got a chance to be." Her eyes go wide again, and they glaze over with the hope and promise of a new beginning as she sees my master plan play out. There are scenes of what could have been and what could be, like she's seeing through time and space. A life with Adam. A life in the Garden. A black-haired boy with stormy gray eyes playing hide and seek between her legs. A black-haired girl with jet black eyes picking ashy petals off of flowers from a sacred bush. And a life dancing in Ilarium with fluffy white-feathered wings and endless music in her head. "Whole," she says with finality. "I want to be whole."

"I can make you whole."

"Yes, Aestrangel. Make me whole again," she says in a faraway voice. She looks off into the distance, beyond the horizon, beyond her Asphodel. She sees into the depths of my manipulated and counterfeit visions and gets lost in the cosmos. For a split second, the face of god flashes into her obsidian eyes, and we both gasp at the same time.

I stand up and face her. She remains on her knees before me. "Are you sure?" I ask.

"Yes," she says, and she bows her head. "Forgive me, Father, for I have sinned..." she begins, and I fan out one of my bladed wings.

With my inner voice, I call to her snakes—I sing to them, and they stand straight up on her head at attention. They extend their long bodies and meet me eye to eye. "You have served her well," I say to them on the inside. "You have served me well too." I thank them for their service and for the years and years of protection they gave to her.

"Oh my God, I am sorry for my sins," Lilith recites. "In choosing to sin and failing to do good, I have sinned against you. I firmly intend, with the help of your grace and mercy, to make up for my sins and to love as I should."

Her confession needs forgiveness, but who am I to be the absolver of sins? I've probably sinned just as much as she has, and I have no real authority to pardon anyone from their transgressions! But I dip my one shoulder forward, poised, and ready to strike. "God the Father of Mercies," I proclaim, "through the death and resurrection of his son, has reconciled the world to himself and sent the holy spirit among us for the forgiveness of sins.

Through his grace, may he give you pardon and bring peace. I absolve you from your sins, in the name of the father, and of the son, and of the holy spirit."

"Amen," she says.

"Go in peace to love and serve the lord," I say, and with one swift motion, my wing slices through the necks of her snakes. Their seven heads fall to the sand, and Lilith's lifeless body tumbles forward at my feet. Apophis makes something like an applause motion on the inside, and I nearly fall over with the strain of his weight within me.

Thunder rolls in the clouds, and thick ropes of lightning jump between them and touch down all around me. It's blinding, and I cower a little, squinting and covering my face with my wings. When the sudden storm ceases, I pull down my wings and look around the shore. Lucifer is here, cradling Lilith in his arms, only it isn't Lucifer, but it is. But it isn't.

*But it is.*

Lucifer is in the soft blue halo of Samael—the name and image Lilith gave him. He has all the features and structures of his Lucifer form, but there's a glow about him, something that is deeply connected to the earth and sky and...

*Humanity.*

Because his angelic essence was too intense for her human mind, he softened himself to be more compatible for her, to be less of an angel and more of a human so her brain could process his presence. I remember in the vision quest that Malek had taken me on, Lilith said to him, "I shall call you Samael because you are the venom of God sent here to poison me with your kisses."

He weeps over her body—great, ear-piercing wails that split the sand dunes in half. He smothers her face in kisses—his lips smack against her stony face with such ferocity as if he's trying to kiss the life back into her. This normally would have been a heart-wrenching and tragic scene of a lost love. I, too, have felt this anguish and despair, and the memories of losing Jake flood into my mind—that feeling of helplessness, that stabbing feeling of pain and sorrow, that feeling of emptiness and abandonment accompanied with the sensation of being utterly lost and out of control. It all grips me too tightly as I watch the Morning Star come undone over Lilith.

But this is not endearing, nor am I empathetic. In fact, I'm quite disgusted. I'm rather appalled by his sniveling and weakness. It's pathetic! Again, I think, *This was who we feared? He was the Big Bad? Look at him now...*

*...he's nothing.*

He doesn't even acknowledge me on the beach; he is too wrapped up in a blanket of his own misery. "Elohim!" he screams with the reverberating voice of a thousand demons. "Why? Why have you blessed me and cursed me at the same time? Why did you even give me life if you were going to show me this death?" Even though his voice is strong and deep with the power of his brethren, his words are pathetic and weak.

Asphodel fades away. The beach fades away. The ocean fades away. The cavern fades away. And all around us, the cosmos opens wide to the great expanse with hundreds of thousands of glittering stars. There is a gravitational pull on my upper body and a tug on my legs as I am suspended in the space of Oblivion between here and nowhere, now, and never. I wrap my arms around my waist instinctively to prevent my body from being split in two. Lucifer's and Lilith's lifeless bodies dangle in the space as well. And from the corner of my eye so does Malek. He hadn't left

Asphodel after all! I reach out my arm to him and him to me, but we are locked in position—held in place by some strong, dynamic force. And now we are here, and I feel a presence—a shining light, a calming peace trying to invade my heart and wiggle its way into my memory and my soul and my being. It tries to light up Apophis with a tiny candle flame, and I fight to keep it out.

"Lucifer," it says in the tongue of the cosmos. "I never left you."

It is the creator hiding behind the shadows but making his presence known and felt. Lucifer looks all around bewilderedly. "But you did. You said you needed me most. You loved me most. But you made them to take my place. And then..." his voice trails as he struggles for the words like he's had this speech rehearsed for a millennia, and now in the face of god, he loses his nerve. "You denied me! Refused me! You sent me to her, and when I showed an ounce of interest in them, you shut me down! Shut me out!"

Lights in the sky flash from white to blue to purple back to white again. "I didn't deny you, Lucifer. I allowed you to find your way." The voice of the lord resonates in my chest, shaking Apophis at his core like a tidal wave swallowing a hundred cities.

"Lilith is my way," Lucifer snivels, and my stomach almost lurches at how pathetic he sounds.

"And you can find your way yet again," the lord says.

"No," Lucifer says. "I have sworn. On life. On death. And on burning sea."

The lights flash brighter in the open expanse, and suddenly from behind a tear in the cosmos, there is a face. A beautiful and hideous face. And I've seen this face before—long ago. The face that haunts me and delights me. There are twisted dark shapes of gnarled bodies and sharp human teeth, and it shines with a light whose color has no name. The mouth of the light can open wide and swallow the heavens and the earth. There is no shape, just images and memories and tales of the entire length of timelessness. It is the face that was reflected in Lilith's eyes before she died—more demon than I remember, more angel than I could have imagined, and more human than I dared to recognize the first time I encountered it. This is the face that condemned me to a life of in-between.

*You are not in-between, Aestrangel,* he says to me, and I stop wriggling in my suspended place.

"Child," he says again to Lucifer. "You are and always have been my Morning Star. It is no secret that I loved you most. But you are not my true opposite. You never were. As the Great Pretender, you have tried, but it was never my intent for you."

Lucifer takes a step away from Lilith. Her body gently floats in the Oblivion, and I realize Lucifer is not locked into place as Malek and I are.

The face breathes in and a swirling hurricane wind dances across the expanse. "In all your guises, in all your forms, even in the corrosion and corruption that is Sataniel, I have loved you, and I will love you still."

Lucifer shakes his head. "I don't believe you!" He screams at the sky and lifts his hand to wave some of his dark magic about himself, but he stops himself and grows still, as if something speaks to him from the inside. As if something whispers and he's trying to hear it clearly.

"Forgive me, Lucifer. Forgive me for what I've done."

Lucifer's eyes sparkle and gleam, and a white light envelopes him from the bottom up. "I do," he says softly, and the light swirls and spirals all around him and all around Lilith wrapping them both in a tornado of mercy and grace and sucking them into the torn face in the Oblivion.

Until they are both gone.

Malek and I are freed from our locked stances. We both fan out our wings and fly to each other for an embrace. But the face is not gone. The face is still there, peeking out from behind a tiny rip in the Oblivion. A thin ray of light from its monster eye winks at us.

"What now?" Malek whispers, and I shrug my shoulders.

"But you are my opposite," the Lord says to me, and I nod. "I stretch the northern sky over empty space and hang the Earth on nothing. I wrap the rain in thick clouds, and the clouds don't burst with the weight. I cover the face of the moon, shrouding it with clouds. I created the horizon when I separated the waters. I set the boundary between day and night. The foundations of heaven tremble; they shudder at my rebuke. By my power, the sea grew calm. By my skill, I crushed the great sea monster. My Spirit made the heavens beautiful, and my power pierced the gliding serpent. These are just a few examples of all that I do, merely a whisper of my power. Who, then, can comprehend the thunder of this power?"

"Me," I respond.

His lights flicker.

"And Camael?" I ask.

"We shall start anew," He responds.

"And Lucifer?"

"It is finished."

"And Apophis?" I ask hesitantly.

"Do with him what you will."

I pause, thinking it over. "And me?"

"You are my Evening Star—the one to follow the Day and bring wrath with her darkness."

"I am sorry," I say, and I don't know why those words left my mouth.

"No. You are not," He answers, and I smile. "You are sorry for the things you have done. But you are not sorry for the things you will do. You are not sorry for what you are to become."

"What am I to become?"

"So much." And the flickering dies away, and the tear closes, and the face of God is gone.

"You will bring a new balance to His existence, ya know," Malek says as he waves his hands. A swirling vortex opens up in the Oblivion to take us back down to Gehenna.

I sigh and mull over his words. *So much.* "That's what He always wanted. That's what He always needed. He chose me to be His true adversary, and I rose to His expectations."

Malek bows his head to me for I am now his true Queen. "I think you exceeded them," he says, taking my hand. "And what of Apophis? There's no need for him now."

"Oh no, dear Malek, you are wrong. There's only one way to show them the true extent of my power and fury. There's only one way to show *all* of them—Daimones, Angelos, Humans—who is taking charge now."

I let go of Malek's hand, close my eyes, and fall back into my consciousness. Apophis is there—the child destroyer stretching and playing and consuming and practically ripping me up from the inside out. But I see now what I have to do. The same way I pulled the power in to me, I have to manipulate it out of me. I have to carve out a section inside for the crux of Apophis while being able to harness that power for use. Because, this thing inside me that I've affectionately given a name and regarded as my child, isn't really a separate entity at all. It's simply me.

He has always been me.

I have always been him.

I call him Apophis.

Together, our name is Aestrangel.

And we are *becoming*.

We are all becoming.

I hold my hands out in front of me to create a black magic orb, but what pulsates and grows is far stronger, far more violent. A ball of fire manifests—black hot flames from earthy rock. I spread my arms out wider and wider as it forms, twists, and develops. And when I can no longer stretch my arms at my sides, I hurl the flaming mass into the Oblivion, into the cosmos, straight at the Creator's most valued design... Earth.

Malek smiles and again guides me to the vortex to go home. "On the eve of the Dark Time, a new deity rises, striking fear into the hearts of believers worldwide," he pronounces.

"The Dark Time," I sigh. "I like the sound of that."

"The humans will now fear the most brutal force to ever terrorize man's every plane of existence, and that fear will replace the notions of love and peace set two millennia ago."

A fireball explodes deep in the cosmos, nearly ripping a hole in the universe.

"The world has shuddered under the shadow of my wings," I say and fall down the vortex with my king at my side.

# BOOK CLUB QUESTIONS:

1. How does the information presented in the prologue shape how you feel about Aestrangel?

2. Discuss Lucifer's plans for Aestrangel. Why do you think this is important to him?

3. How do you feel about Aestrangel's relationship with Malek? Are they truly meant for each other, or is Aestrangel using him for her own benefit? A little bit of both? If this storyline was told from Malek's perspective, how might it be different?

4. Was Aestrangel justified in her actions? Why or why not?

5. Most characters in literature go through a hero's journey; their journey takes them on an experience that is life-altering, and the character eventually makes the ultimate sacrifice for the greater good or returns home with new power or knowledge. Such is not the case for Aestrangel.

In fact, it is just the opposite, as Aestrangel ventures on her own path—the villain's journey. Thinking back to book 1 to the end of book 3, what major beats mapped out Aestrangel as the most supreme villain? When did her downfall begin? When was her point of no return? When did you realize she could no longer be saved?

6. What is symbolic about Apophis? What hell do you think it unleashed upon the world?

7. Aestrangel has three very important encounters with three important biblical figures: Adam, Cain, and Jesus. Do her encounters with them align with what you know about biblical history?

8. Aestrangel jockeyed herself into Lucifer's position as Lucifer's true motivations are revealed. Do your feelings for the Dark Lord change after realizing the reasons for his behavior? Why or why not?

9. Ultimately, the driving force behind the entire story is love. What types of love are most evident in this last installment?

10. You've finished the series. Now go back and reread the prologue in the context of an epilogue. Have your feelings/thoughts/perceptions changed about Aestrangel?

# AUTHOR BIO

**M**aria DeVivo writes horror and dark fantasy for both YA and adult audiences. Each of her series has been Amazon best-sellers and has won multiple awards since 2012. When not writing, she teaches Language Arts and Journalism to middle school students in Florida. A lover of all things dark and demented, the worlds she creates are fantastical and immersive. Get swept away in the lands of elves, zombies, angels, demons, and witches (but not all in the same place). Maria takes great pleasure in warping the comfort factor in her readers' minds, and just when you think you've reached a safe space in her stories, she snaps you back into her twisted reality.

# Fantasy

**D. Lambert**
To Walk into the Sands
Rydan
Celebrant
Northlander
Esparan
King
Traitor
His Last Name

**J.M. Paquette**
Klauden's Ring
Solyn's Body
The Inbetween
Hannah's Heart

**Lou Kemp**
The Violins Played Before Junstan
Music Shall Untune the Sky

**R.J. Young**
Challenges of Tawa

**Sydney Wilder**
Daughter of Serpents

**Valerie Willis**
Cedric: The Demonic Knight
Romasanta: Father of Werewolves
The Oracle: Keeper of the
Gaea's Gate
Artemis: Eye of Gaea
King Incubus: A New Reign

**Kyle Sorrell**
Munderworld
Potarium

**Discover more at
4HorsemenPublications.com**

www.ingramcontent.com/pod-product-compliance
Lightning Source LLC
Chambersburg PA
CBHW061250310726
48971CB00007B/2296